A BRIDGE OF HER OWN

A New Adult Novel

CAREY HEYWOOD

Carey Heywood LLC

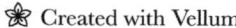 Created with Vellum

Mom,
you are my lighthouse.

Chapter One

There is a quiet insecurity in all of us. A person terrified of public speaking. Someone who always wonders what people will think of her if she says the wrong thing or makes a mistake. So how is it a girl like this is standing in the center of a University basketball court, at half time, a mic in her hand the crowded stadium listening to her every word?

Two months prior to the spectacle at the basketball court Jane was leaving work. 'Ugh', she thought. It was a sticky hot August afternoon. She slid into her four door sedan. Her sunglasses fogged up as she cracked the windows and cranked her air conditioning. She twisted her shoulder length brown hair into a bun. At least the day was over. She shared a townhouse style two story apartment with a girlfriend. The apartment only came with one reserved parking spot, so part of Jane's daily routine was trying to beat her neighbors to one of the open spots in the lot.

She was home in no time and called out to her roommate "Honey I'm home" as she kicked off her shoes and dropped her keys in a table by the door.

Her roommate Lacey was perched on their sofa her feet up on the coffee table hunched over painting her toenails. She was using a bright glittery purple and was adding neon green polka dots. Tame for Lacey. Jane's orange tabby was curled in a ball at the other end of the sofa. He would lift his head and look at Lacey whenever she made the sofa cushions move.

"Simmer down Ronald" she fussed at him.

They had a love hate relationship. It had been a long week. Probably the busiest since tax season had ended, or maybe she was just tired now that summer was over. All Jane wanted to do was curl on the sofa and catch up on her dvr queue. Lacey however had other ideas and promised to do dishes for the next two weeks if Jane would go out.

Lacey wanted to check out a new bar, she heard was owned by a former boy band star. Jane just hoped a rum and coke there would not cost more than a DVD. Lacey got all dressed up. She wore a fun multi colored dress and some heels her poor toes may never forgive her for. But she was on the shorter side and heels were a daily must wear in her mind.

Jane opted for a khaki shirt dress and brown sandals. She pulled her hair back in a low pony. Lacey wore her blonde bob styled with the ends curling up versus under. Jane went neutral with her makeup and Lacey bold with green eye shadow. She scratched Ronald behind the ears, making him purr a guttural sound from his throat.

"Be a good watch kitty" Jane said with a kiss on his nose before she left.

The bar was pretty packed for how early it was. The girls found a table and ordered a couple of drinks and fries to munch on in lieu of dinner. Then proceeded to people watch. The music was on the loud side so they had to shout their conversation. There was a group of guys in suits next to them. Jane guessed they had come for happy hour and were still here. They looked very relaxed with their loosened ties.

A couple of them were trying to catch Lacey and Jane's attention. One brave soul had even asked Lacey if she would like to dance. While she would normally be all for it, this bar did not have a dance floor and she had not drunk enough to be okay with that yet. She turned him down with a smile. Jane observed one guy chuckling to himself at his friend striking out with Lacey. He looked up and caught her watching him. She blushed and looked away.

Lacey witnessed this exchange and boldly introduced herself to this guy and dragged him over to meet Jane, then took off to the bathroom, or so she claimed.

"Traitor" Jane muttered to herself.

She was not very good at talking to strangers, let alone cute strangers of the opposite sex. His name was Gabe. He was tall and had a lanky build. In the dim light of the bar his hair looked either dark blonde or light brown. Jane wasn't sure and she was guessing his eyes were brown. It was around the time she was deciding that she thought he had a cute smile when she also realized she had not said a word to him yet.

"Ahhhh" oh Lord what to say "umm...so are you having fun?" was all she could come up with.

"Sure" he shouted "this place is cool, it's the first time I've ever been here."

"Me too!" Jane replied happy to have not only broken the ice but having something in common as well.

It turned out one of Gabe's friends bar tended there. Jane explained how Lacey wanted to come to possibly run into a celebrity and she was along for moral support.

"Oh yeah I guess some famous guy owns the place."

Wondering where Lacey was, Jane looked around and finally spied her over by the bar waving and giving Jane a double thumbs up. Lacey was lucky Gabe was so cute; otherwise Jane could have killed her for deserting her. Gabe sat in Lacey's empty stool after Jane confessed she could barely hear him. As he sat down they bumped knees. They both started to apologize and laughed as they tried to speak at the same time. They both fell silent as they each waited for the other.

"Alright, I'll go first. So tell me about yourself." Gabe said.

Jane was suddenly tongue tied again. "Uhhhh, I just got out of school a couple years ago…err college, not high school…" Why did she say that! Of course he would know she meant college. She cringed. "I work for an accountant and share a place with Lacey who you met earlier. You?" Whew.

Jane was actually holding a conversation with a stranger and had not said anything too silly.

"My name is Gabe, as you already know because I told you that before…" Was he nervous too? Jane wondered "I am a history teacher and am spending a lot of time right now renovating a total fixer upper. No roommate other than my dog but I'm not sure anyone would want the live with me, given the state my house is in."

"Bummed summer is over?" Jane asked.

"It's a toss up" Gabe smiled "it gives me an excuse not to work on the house." A waitress came up and Gabe asked Jane if she would like another drink.

"Sure, a rum and coke please" Jane replied.

Lacey returned at that point and whispered on Jane's ear "You good?"

Jane grinned and Lacey went to go talk to Gabe's

4

friends. Their drinks arrived and Jane daintily sipped hers after thanking Gabe. Lacey returned and informed them that once they were done with their drinks, the whole group was heading over to a dance club down the street. Lacey beamed while Jane panicked. Jane was a terrible dancer so, as far as she was concerned there goes anything with Gabe. They downed their drinks and the group all headed towards the club.

Jane and Gabe hung to the back of the group and chatted along the way. One of Gabe's friends, Matt, joined them and began to tell Jane, somewhat intoxicatedly, what a great guy Gabe was. Jane actually felt a rush when she noticed him blush at the compliments and quickly change the subject to ask Matt how his folks were.

Matt, not easily deterred, went on to tell Jane how even his parents loved Gabe and thought he was a great guy. Jane brought her hand up to cover her mouth and suppress a giggle.

"Thanks dude" Gabe grumbled.

"So" Matt asked "have you told her about your Baby?"

Oh God Jane thought he has a baby! Just my luck I meet a nice guy and I didn't even consider he may be married or have a girlfriend.

"I already told Jane I have a dog, I have not told her that my dog's name is Baby." A dog!!! Jane loved dogs. "I got her from a neighbor who was moving and could not take her and had an unhealthy Dirty Dancing fixation."

"I have a cat" Jane grinned "his name is Ronald and he is very spoiled."

"Ronald, that's a different name for a cat" Gabe said.

"He's orange" Jane said as though that would clearly make sense.

"Harry Potter?" Gabe asked getting it.

She nodded enthusiastically. With that they were at the

club. Lacey headed straight for the dance floor and started tearing it up. Gabe and Jane found a table and ordered some drinks. Then came the question Jane was dreading

"Would you like to dance?" Before she could answer Lacey shimmied over with a waitress who was carrying a tray full of shots.

Oh Lord, Jane had reached her limit and opted for an ice water instead. She excused herself to the Ladies and grabbed Lacey on the way.

"Oh my God Lace, he is sooooo cute" she gushed as she applied a fresh coat of lip gloss "What should I do?, Should I ask for his number or wait for him to ask for mine? Oh and I may never forgive you for suggesting dancing!"

"Jane, you are not a bad dancer, besides it's too crowded out there to do anything other than shuffle around. Dance with him, that way you'll have an excuse to touch him."

"Touch him? That sounds so dirty" Jane giggled.

"I'm not telling you to take him home with you, just dance. Now hurry up we've been in here too long" Lacey said.

They headed back to the table and about halfway there saw a group of girls talking with Gabe and his friends

Lacey saw Jane stiffen and said "relax, he's into you. I can tell."

Either way, it made Jane feel self conscious and maybe a tinge jealous. Yikes! Jealous, she just met this guy, ugh.

"Jane!" Gabe called leaving the group "let's dance" he grabbed her hand and led her to the dance floor.

She felt simultaneously thrilled and terrified at the same time. Lacey was right, he liked her back! There was an upbeat song she recognized from the radio playing.

Once on the dance floor they stood facing each other and Jane froze.

"Okay?" Gabe asked concerned.

"I suck at dancing" Jane whispered embarrassed.

"That all?" Gabe grinned and held out his hand.

She took it and he placed his other on her hip and pulled her too him. She could feel the heat coming from his hand through the material of her dress. She placed her other hand on his shoulder. He was very firm for his lanky build. She could smell his cologne and it smelled really good, kind of earthy and masculine. He led them to the music and Jane caught Lacey's eye over his shoulder and tried not to giggle as she yet again gave her double thumbs up. Gabe followed her gaze and saw Lacey who though caught tried to play it off and talk to the guy next to her.

"Hmm I've earned not a single but a double thumbs up, that has got to be a good sign" he remarked.

Not sure of how to respond Jane nodded. Once the song was over they headed back to the group. Gabe did not let go of her hand and his friends noticed. He received cat calls and pats on the back. He hung his head and apologized to Jane saying his friends were so embarrassing and he would not be surprised if they serenaded her with either the 'lost that loving feeling song' from Top Gun or the old elementary school fall back 'kissing in the tree.'

Lacey came to their rescue "Oh grow up and leave them alone, it's late. Who wants to go grab food?"

Chapter Two

F ood ended up being a very popular idea. The debate began with where to go and location won out as they all headed to a local dinner within walking distance. Once there the lights seems extra bright in comparison to the dim bar and dance club. Jane and Lacey hit the ladies room to perform a quick hair/make up check.

"So has he asked for your number yet?" Lacey asked.

"No, is that bad?" Jane said feeling suddenly insecure.

"Please, I'm sure he will. He is totally into you." Lacey assured her. "Let's go, I'm starving."

Jane sat down next to Gabe and ordered a Belgian waffle and a cherry coke. Gabe went with a Western Omelet which Jane secretly hoped was light on the onions. While they waited, Gabe took out his cell phone put his arm around her and snapped a picture of them.

"Going to text that picture to your mom, dude?" Matt called out from the other end of the table.

"No bro, just wanted a pic to go with the number" then looking at Jane, "if she'll give it to me. That is I would completely understand why she wouldn't, given I hang out with the likes of you." He raised his eyebrow and said "So, what do you say? Can I call you sometime?"

Jane felt the color rush to her cheeks as all of the eyes at the table were suddenly on her. "I'd like that."

"Whew" Gabe exclaimed pretending to wipe sweat of his brow "that would have really blown if you had said no."

She gave him her number, then he texted her the picture so she would also have his number. She sipped her cherry coke as she tried to decide if the feeling in her gut was hunger or butterflies or maybe even a combination of the two. It didn't help that every time Gabe wasn't looking Lacey was either mouthing 'Oh My God' or winking at her.

Once the food came and Jane dug in and then she knew for sure it was butterflies. While they ate, Lacey kept everyone rolling with stories from her job as a temp. Who knew stuffing envelopes could be so funny? Once Jane finished her waffle, she was struggled not to yawn. Didn't matter how excited she was to meet Gabe, she was tired. Not fair she thought and contemplated ordering coffee.

Gabe picked up on it and asked "Sleepy?"

"I'm sorry, I don't usually stay out this late."

"No worries, it's really late for me too" he said stifling a yawn.

Lacey was the only one asking about an after party.

"Lace, I'm beat. Let's call it a night" Jane pleaded.

"Did you drive, or could you use a lift?" Gabe asked.

"We would love a lift!" Lacey shouted.

"Please ignore her, we drove" Jane said shaking her head "I'm parked over by the bar we met at"

"Me too" Gabe replied "Matt and I can walk you to your car."

He held her hand on the walk back. Lacey and Matt

walked ahead of them. Lacey barefoot swinging her heels from her hands as she walked. Matt informing her she may catch the plague from germs on the sidewalk. From that point on Lacey kept trying to touch him with her feet. Gabe and Jane, laughing as Matt, ran from Lacey to avoid the plague.

Once at Jane's car she blanked on what to say. Would he kiss her in front of his friend? What should she do, say? Lacey, suddenly and somewhat suspiciously exhausted, got into the car and was sound asleep. With his friend waiting off by his car Gabe pulled Jane into his arms and gave her a long hug.

Into her ear her murmured "I really didn't even want to go out tonight but man I am really happy I did and that we met, Jane."

He pulled away from her and opened her door for her. Once she was in, he patted the top of her car before walking back over to his friend.

"Drive safe!" Jane called out to him.

She grimaced instantly feeling as though she could have said something cooler. He turned back towards her and grinned. Once they were out of the parking lot Lacey popped right up and smiled.

"You owe me so much for taking you out. Man he was really cute. Tell me everything I may have missed from the beginning."

Jane spent the whole car ride home revisiting every look, touch and word spoken with Gabe, for Lacey. Ronald greeted them at the door loudly protesting his empty water dish. After filling it she floated into her pjs and brushed her teeth and passed out, thankful she could sleep in. Jane's eyelids fluttered as patch of sunlight moved right over her eyes.

She prayed for clouds to block out the sun, pulled her

blanket over her head and went back to sleep. The smell of coffee an hour or so later finally roused her. Lacey was flipping through the TV line up, coffee in hand, sprawled out on the sofa. Jane went to make herself a cup then picking up Ronald plopped down with him into their armchair.

"Man, last night was a good night. Do you think Gabe will call you today?" Lacey asked not looking away from the TV.

"I hope so" Jane replied inhaling that glorious coffee scent. "He was really nice and all as far as I can tell but I still feel kinda silly liking a guy I met at a bar."

"Please" Lacey started looking at her "it's not like you sucked face all night and never even found out his name. Yeah, cause that was me last month. It would be nice to run into him again though, he was a kick ass kisser whoever he was."

They ate toasted bagels and topped with cream cheese and watched reruns.

"So, what's on tap today?" Lacey asked.

"I have crazy laundry to get through and I promised I'd run by my parents house to show my mom how to print pictures with her new camera. Wanna come?"

"Got nothing better to do" Lacey answered standing.

One perk about apartment living, multiple washing machines. Jane was able to do 3 loads and Lacey 2 loads all at the same time. Once their clothes were cleaned and put away they headed to Jane's parents house.

Chapter Three

H er parents still lived in the house Jane had grown up in. She usually saw them twice a month or more depending on how busy she was. Jane's dad was out front mowing the lawn. Every year he got closer to retirement, the more preoccupied he seemed with their curb appeal. Today for example he was practicing cutting the grass in a diamond shape pattern with the lawn mower. He waved as the girls pulled up but continued his task.

"I see your dad is still working on having the best lawn on the block" Lacey observed.

"Isn't your dad into bird watching now?" Jane returned eyebrow raised.

"Touché" Lacey giggled. They entered through the side door and dropped their purses on the kitchen table Jane calling out

"Mom, where are you?"

"We're in the living room" her mother returned.

'We?' Jane mouthed to Lacey as the girls made their way to the living room.

Jane came to an abrupt stop in the doorway once she

realized who was with her mom. Lacey, not expecting the halt, plowed into Jane sending both girls stumbling into the room.

"How graceful" Mrs. Martin observed from her perch on the loveseat.

Next to her sat Jane's ex boyfriend Wyatt Huntington III.

"Oh um, sorry" Jane mumbled looking down at her sweat pants tucked into Ugg boots and faded cookie monster t-shirt she sometimes slept in.

It was the perfect look to run into an old boyfriend she thought. She could tell by the look on her mother's face that she felt the same way. Wyatt looked very respectable in pressed beige pants and a crisp white oxford.

"Mom, you should have called and let me know Wyatt was stopping by."

"Darling," her mother sighed "Wyatt stopped by so unexpectedly" then turning to him "though it was such a welcome surprise."

Lacey was not thrilled to see Wyatt and coolly sat in an armchair and stared at him. Jane had met Lacey first in college and then Wyatt. She had actually introduced Jane to Wyatt. Lacey had also been Jane's first real friend. Before that, Jane's only real companion was her mother. Her father Mitch traveled quite a lot for work when she was little.

Jane was a slight child with long brown hair and big brown eyes, and was very reserved for a child. When Jane was very young her mother would receive compliments on how well behaved she was. Mothers at play groups or babysitters would say how lucky she was to have such a perfect little angel.

They would pepper her for advice making her the center of attention in their mommy and me groups. Her mother glowed under the compliments and nourished these ideals to a fault. She was an only child and her mother was a stay at home mom. Her first true daily interaction with children came when she began kindergarten. She adored school but was very quiet and shy around her classmates.

She had grown up in the West End of Richmond Virginia. While booming with neighborhoods and businesses today, when she was a child it was fairly rural. Her parent's owned a classic colonial style home with green siding and black shutters. Her mother was the neighborhood garden snob with her Kentucky blue grass and prominent flowerbeds. They normally experienced all four seasons though some winters they did not get any snow. Jane liked fall and spring the best. All of the leaves changing colors and the vibrant blooms of new buds.

Her family would go downtown when going out to eat. There was an area called the fan with fun restaurants and boutiques. Her mother was very social and she would go with her most days for lunch with the ladies during summer and school breaks. She would sit primly at the table with the grown up's, because she was so well behaved so she was always the only child who could come.

At the bus stop for school she would lose herself in the beauty around her. She was oblivious to the other children from her street. Her teachers were sweet but did not push her to interact with the other children. She was content to sit back and observe. Jane had been taught by her mother to speak only when spoken to and that it was preferred for children to be seen and not heard.

Jane would sit in the cavity between their sofa and bay window of their living room to observe the goings on of her street. Sitting with her feet curled beneath her, she would watch the kids from her street when they played outside. Her dainty nose inches from the window, she saw them play and jump in puddles on rainy days and run through sprinklers on hot summer days. She was aware of her mother's opinion of the neighborhood youth. She did not favor them.

Jane however thought they were wonderful and would day dream of the adventures they could have. One particularly muddy day, one of these children braved the well manicured walkway of the Martin's home to inquire if Jane could come out and play. They were making mud pies she happily told Jane's mother. Jane cringed knowing what her mother's response would be. What agony she felt at that moment, she knew after her mother was finished with this little girl another invitation to play would be unlikely.

Jane observed her mother wrinkle her nose in disgust. She looked up and down at the filthy tyke on her doorstep. The young girl seemed to shrink under her gaze. She then informed the young girl that Jane was not the type of little girl to play in the mud and to run along. That was the last time any of her neighbors came over to ask Jane to play.

That evening Jane practiced wrinkling her nose in the mirror as she had seen her mother do. As she daintily fluffed her ruffled skirt, she wistfully imagined making a mud pie. From that point on she would imagine she was part of the group. The fun things, she dreamed they had done, filled her afternoons. With her eyes closed and head leaned against the back of their sofa she was content.

Her father traveled for work when she was younger and was gone sometimes a week at a time. Jane wished he was home more often. He, like her, was the quiet sort. Even though he did not come right out and say it she knew he adored her. He would always bring a state spoon home for her from his travels.

She treasured her collection and had a display case of

them in her room. When he was gone and she felt lonely she would hold the spoon from whatever state he was in that trip and rub the handle. Sometimes she would sleep with that spoon under her pillow. It made her feel as though he was not as far away.

While most of her classmates went to school in blue jeans or corduroy pants and t-shirts Jane was dressed in a skirt and blouse or a dress every day. Her fingernails were always painted a pale shade of pink, and any chips to her nail polish not tolerated. Jane had piano lessons and was not permitted to join such outdoor activities as girl scouts or soccer. She wistfully listened to the little girls of her school discuss earning badges and selling cookies.

Sitting alone each day at the lunch table Jane felt so isolated. Sometimes a classmate would move her way and she would look up hopeful but all too often they were just passing her to sit somewhere else. She brought her lunch from home. Each day instead of a normal paper napkin she had fancy linen. She wished she could just buy lunch like the other students but her mother enjoyed making her lunches. Each day she would leave a note for Jane, in French.

Her classmates considered her to be a snob because she never spoke to anyone and was always so dressed up. Children can be cruel. While they shunned her most of the time, from time to time they would even pick on her further to attempt to elicit a reaction from her. They would crowd around her tugging at her hair taunting "Plain Jane." She never reacted in front of them but would cry and hug herself in a stall of the girl's restroom when no one else was there.

The teasing eventually escalated physically to her being pushed around as well, usually from behind. She would fall, rip her tights and dirty her hands. Her mother would rail at her over her state of appearance after these events. She was deaf to Jane's attempt to tell her what happened. Once so distraught over her lack of friends, she confided to her father tears streaming down her face.

"Janey anyone would be crazy not to like you" he soothed.

Her mother who was eavesdropping announced those girls were simply jealous but promptly enrolled Jane in a small all girls private school. Unfortunately, many of her new classmates had already been attending the school together for years. Since Jane was too shy to put herself out there she was doomed to repeat her experience from her last school.

However, since the school was so small, with fewer students to keep watch over, her teachers were very observant. This gave any would-be bullies less opportunity to strike. Also, since there were uniforms at this school, she wasn't thought a snob for the clothes she wore. She would lose herself in books as a way to past time. Mostly it was just Jane and her parents.

She would have loved a cat or a dog but her mother was allergic to both. Caving, her father finally got her a goldfish. She loved her little goldfish, Watson named for one of her favorite characters, the doctor from Sherlock Holmes. His bowl lived on her bedside table. In the dim glow of her clock radio she would talk to him at night before she fell asleep. He was a good fish but she really craved a pet she could snuggle close during rough times.

As she grew there were times she would catch her mother observing her with a very satisfied look on her face. There was something in these looks that Jane was able to tell that she was doing everything just right. There were other times though. If Jane brought home a B on a school-work assignment or during awkward times if her skin broke out or when she needed braces it was clear that her mother was disappointed. These times made Jane feel miserable as all she ever wanted was to make her mother happy.

Her father was always content with her company. When he was not travelling on business she would gravitate to him. In the evening after dinner she would sit and watch National Geographic with him in the den while her mother watched her shows in the living room. These were the most peaceful times Jane remembered from growing up. She was able to relax.

Otherwise, she turned her homework in on time and was a favorite among her teachers. She just seemed to be lacking a spark of interest in anything. Each day was the same as the next. As the years passed and their schooling evolved Jane began to find enjoyment in her Art classes. There was something liberating, after learning the basic method they were free to decide subject, color and any variation of the end output for their work.

She especially loved to draw. Charcoal to pad she would portray her life how she wished it was. She was riding a bike or surfing with dolphins flanking her. Inspired Jane would lose herself in books chronicling the lives and works of her favorite artists. It stuck her that someone as famous and well liked as Picasso for example could use shapes that in no way resembled those of a human figure to create a human figure.

The concept that even while the shapes were so far from symmetrical, not only she but the masses at large found beauty in the imperfection created. She even attempted to deconstruct objects in her own drawings. She particularly enjoyed the idea that different styles and formats of artwork spoke to people differently. That one painting could hold so many different stories.

She quietly passed through her remaining years at school. When the time came to select a college or university her eyes wandered far away from home. Her mother however would not consider her perfect innocent daughter going so far away. She was given the choice between 3 in state schools, all within a 2 hour drive from home. Her initial thought process was to pick the one furthest from home and call it a day but after deeper study of the different programs available at each she in the end selected the closest.

It had the best Art History program. Jane's mother did not care what she studied as long as it wasn't anything bohemian like Women's Studies or masculine like Engineering in her opinion. Besides her mother believed it wasn't as though Jane would ever work for a living. She was clearly destined to marry a future CEO or politician. There was nothing undesirable about studying Art History as long as she wouldn't become or date an artist, her mother thought.

Besides, it would be the perfect excuse to take a family trip that summer to Europe, that way Jane could see some of what she was studying, in person. What professor wouldn't appreciate a scholar who was world traveled. Jane wasn't even accepted yet and her mother was already contemplating how she could assist her daughter in maintaining her perfect image. Jane mentally counted the days till graduation. She was accepted to her first choice school and was thrilled to learn of her mother's planned vacation.

With her parents in tow, she blissfully toured the finest museums of Europe. They spent three separate days touring the Louvre in Paris, well at least Jane did. Her father bowed out after the first day claiming an aching knee. Her mother gave up after the second day. She could not understand Jane's manic desire to see everything but acknowledged that this was an appropriate desire giving her course of study. So, while her father napped and her mother shopped on the third day Jane floated from exhibit to exhibit all by herself.

There were some wonderful museums in her home-town but this was the most famous museum in the world. She breathed in the spirit of artists long since gone but immortal through their work. She imagined Masters of their craft embracing their creations and wondered what it would be like to touch something Da Vinci or Van Gough did. She would never actually risk it, but at one point in the day, sat on a bench in front of the 'The Bathers' by Renoir and visualized tracing her fingertip over every swell and stroke of color.

The rest of their trip flew by and she was shopping and packing for school before she knew it.

Chapter Four

Moving into her new dorm room and meeting her new roommate was surreal. Her new roommate Trisha was certifiably insane. She looked normal enough but upon actually entering their dorm room realized that was far from the truth. She had a collection of doll heads. Actual doll heads, no bodies anywhere to be seen. She had them displayed in a shadow box already hung above her bed. Jane distressed, looked from her mother to her father with her eyes wide. Jane could not live with her. She honestly wasn't sure if it was safe for anyone to live with her.

Her parents were in complete agreement and took Jane to see the dorm rep of that floor. There was a short line of other unhappy dorm dwellers already waiting. This is where Jane first met Lacey. Lacey's roommate was an avid taxidermist. Lacey an animal (living) lover could not deal with this. Jane's father laughed and told Lacey about Jane's roommate and the doll heads.

Lacey looked Jane up and down and decided she could not be any crazier than her current roommate and negotiated a prisoner exchange. Lacey in appearance was opposite of Jane. Lacey was incredible in action convincing each of their current roommates that they were perfect for each other. At one point even suggesting her roommate use the doll heads in her taxidermy. Jane had to bite her lips to avoid laughing out loud. Lacey was not phased by Jane's shyness. She figured if they were going to live together Jane would eventually warm up to her and decided she should do it sooner rather than the alternative. Jane found her absolutely refreshing.

They, of course had their moments. Jane tended to bottle up her frustrations till she made herself sick while Lacey would blow her top, when in a mood, for little reason at all. Early on they set ground rules for what was expected of each other. Lacey let her know that she was not a mind reader and Jane HAD to come to her if she was ever doing something that bothered her. Jane also asked that Lacey not entertain suitors in their dorm room because let's face it there are some things you can't un-see.

Navigating the unknown waters of their first weeks of their freshman year together was a bonding experience. Their schedules were very similar. Most days they would skip the cafeteria breakfast and opt for milk and cereal instead. Keeping their small dorm fridge stocked made Jane feel grown up. Which was funny, Lacey teased her, considering her favorite cereal was the very grown up Fruit Loops.

Most evenings they would stay in studying but Lacey was able to coax Jane out on average one day a week. Happy to people watch Jane was really enjoying herself. Her mother was shocked that she was not coming home on the weekends given how close they lived. Part of the reason was she did not have a car since it was discouraged for freshman students. She didn't want to have her father come pick her up and then have to drop her back off again even though she was certain he would not have minded.

The other reason not surprisingly was that she was enjoying her independence. It also gave her an opportunity to get to know Lacey better. Part of her was dumbstruck that Lacey would elect to spend her free time with her. Lacey, while new to the area as well as the school, had no shortage of new friends. She just seemed to like Jane the best and as long as Jane was willing she was always welcomed if not encouraged out with her.

Jane had no idea what Lacey saw in her. What she did not know was most of Lacey's bombastic bravado came from disguising how similar they really were. She had learned how to overcome her shyness and felt protective of Jane. Lacey was originally from the mid west and had selected their school also for its art program. Not art history like Jane, her course of study was Theatre Arts. Given her lack of ties to the area Jane was curious why this program had appealed to her. It turned out the University's Professors were renowned and many previous graduates of the program were fairly successful. So leaving her parents in Iowa she set out on her own.

By the end of that semester they were very in tune to their unique ticks. Lacey even went home with Jane for the holidays. She could have gone home to Iowa but her folks were going on a couples cruise to the Caribbean. They had invited her to go along but who wants to be the third wheel of that? Jane's folks lived half an hour from their school. Lacey had never met anyone like Jane, so quiet and seemingly without ulterior motive in her friendship. Neither having a sibling, they formed a bond not unlike sisterhood. Lacey felt protective of Jane and stepped into the big sister role. Jane was the kindest soul she had ever met and she could not wait to meet her parents. Lacey could tell her dad was pretty laid back while her mom seemed wound a bit tightly. She fussed at Jane in ways Lacey could tell was driving her crazy so she suggested Jane give her a tour of the neighborhood.

"So why do you let your mom jump all over you like that?" Lacey asked once they were out of earshot in the driveway.

Jane shrugged "What else am I supposed to do?"

"Um how about telling her you are an adult legally able to vote so it is unnecessary for her to still know the time of your last cycle or examine your teeth so she can decide if you have been flossing or not?" Lacey retorted.

"I think she would have a heart attack if I ever said anything like that to her" Jane giggled.

"I really think you should try setting some sort of boundaries though" Lacey went on "Otherwise she will walk all over you your whole life."

Jane knew Lacey was right but it was her mom. Yes, she did feel as though she had to do things that she did not want to do around her but aren't most parents like that?

It was chilly but the sun was out so they took a pleasant lap around Jane's block. Since it was still light out none of the houses had their holiday lights turned on yet. Jane pointed out landmarks along the way. Pool down that road, home of the first boy she ever dreamed of kissing, where the stupid lady who never cleans up after her dog leaved. There was a bench at the end of the block, on a grassy hill. They sat for a spell enjoying the crisp air. On the way back Lacey said it was a bummer they would not see any of the houses lit up.

"Let's go on a tacky light tour!" Jane exclaimed.

"The what?" Lacey replied.

"It's a route that you take past all of the WAY decorated houses" Jane answered "You'll love it."

Jane's parents declined the invitation to come along. After supper they bundled up and with a map printed from Jane's dad's computer they set off. On the way Jane told Lacey she someday dreamed of taking the tour by limo, as some companies in town that annually did that. As they drove neighborhood to neighborhood checking out light display after light display they found themselves at the mother of all over decorated houses they had even seen.

There were two houses side by side that had jointly decorated every inch of available lawn and roof space. The girls parked and braving the cold weather walked up to take a closer look, as many other people also appeared to be doing. A homeowner was offering cups of hot cocoa to everyone and holiday music played in the background. There was also a donation box set up with proceeds going to a local charity.

"This is the most amazing thing I have ever seen" Lacey said awestruck.

Christmas morning Jane presented her parents with an Oil painting of the Arc de Triumph she had done as a homage of their trip to France. Her father gushed over it while her mother continued to ask if she had met any nice boys. Her father shook his head and joked she should wait until she was thirty. Lacey and Jane exchanged their presents to each other.

Jane had gotten Lacey a monthly subscription to her favorite fashion magazine and a husband pillow as Lacey coveted Jane's. Lacey gave Jane a calendar from the Louvre and silver charm bracelet with a charm. The charm was a small heart with BFF engraved on it. Jane was truly touched and close to tears as she hugged Lacey in thanks.

From that trip on the two were inseparable. They navigated the ups and downs of college life together. Lacey, with the hope of someday ending up on Broadway or even in Hollywood. Jane was her always willing audience and sometimes coach helping her learn lines. It was amazing how Lacey's course of study also impacted Jane's personality.

Jane studied with the dream of someday being a curator of a museum the constant repetition of speaking out loud with Lacey while running lines with her, gave Jane additional confidence in her own courses to occasionally raise her hand in response to a professor's question. Prior to her friendship with Lacey this would have been completely out of character for her.

Chapter Five

Jane invited Lacey to come stay with her and her family for a couple of months while she worked on a production at the local theatre. Lacey did not have a leading role but it was a paying gig (minimum wage). She would not have been able to afford staying had it not been for Jane's parents. Jane's dad especially got a kick out of Lacey's antics while Jane's mom secretly prayed Lacey would not rub too much off on Jane.

Jane with her art background also became involved in Lacey's production as she helped build and decorate the various set backdrops. They both had a blast, and would be able to refer to their summer work during their next term. On sold out nights Jane would sit with the audio crew and watch the show from the catwalk. It was a beautiful view high above the audience. Some of her favorite memories came from her quiet perch. If there was better light up there, it would be a fun place to sketch she mused. Unfortunately, it was so dark she would be completely unable to see what she was drawing. It was good practice though to try, and once back at their dorm room recall from memory something she had previously witnessed.

For Jane it was wonderful to have someone at home to split the attention with. Her mother seemed less inclined to correct her when Lace was around. Also, Lacey seemed to notice when her mother was about pick at Jane and would change the subject or ask Mrs. Martin to help her with something. They could also borrow her dad's car and tool around town, usually to the fan, where they would park and window shop up and down Cary Street. For Jane, she was for the first time in her life feeling somewhat adult around her parents.

Before starting their sophomore year Jane went home with Lacey to Iowa for a couple of weeks to, now, meet her parents. She was particularly excited to meet Lacey's mother, as she was an actual working artist. She was very eccentric and could easily be described as a hippie. Her current medium was found material that she would then assemble and paint. There was a large painted structure of lawn chairs welded to baby strollers and artificial tabletop Christmas trees in their front yard. Lacey rolled her eyes as they approached it.

"I wish she would go back to pottery" Lacey sighed walking up "that took up way less space."

Lacey's father on the other hand managed a local wellness center and spa. Lacey and Jane helped out for a couple of days in exchange for a spa day.

"We have got to come visit your parents more often" Jane said from her seaweed wrap.

"Just gotta remember to keep moving or we might end up part of my mom's next sculpture" Lacey joked from her mud bath. It really was a peaceful trip but Jane did notice that Lacey's mom when 'inspired,' was not really there for Lacey.

She mused to herself that if you combined her hover mom with Lacey's flighty mom you might just come up with the perfect combination of interested disinterest. Returning to campus as a team was so refreshing versus all of the unknowns of their previous year. Again they shared a room and took pains to match their schedules up for classes. Over the summer they even bought all of their bedding together so it would coordinate. Lacey also shipped down a painting her mother had done. It was based off of a photo of Jane and Lacey from their trip.

This year they actually had one class together. A prerequisite math course neither of them were looking forward to. That is until their professor walked in. He could have been a model for an Italian underwear designer. Math went from their least favorite subject to suddenly their favorite. Lacey took pains to look flawless for each class. Jane teased her even though she had to admit if it was a math class day she did tend to wear jeans instead of sweats. Otherwise their year was flying by.

Lacey dated a guy named Anthony on and off one semester. He was an exchange student from Spain. Neither really understood anything the other was saying. It was mainly a physical relationship. When he left to return to Spain she was really bummed having decided he was the ideal mate. They spent their winter break at Jane's again. A night, a few days before Christmas, they drove to the house that had all of the decorations again. They decided it would be their winter ritual.

The second semester seemed to race by, each busy with their courses. Lacey was trying to work on her Irish accent nonstop. It was like living with a leprechaun, Jane teased. Her accent was improving though. Someone who lived on their floor had even asked Jane about the new Irish chick. Lacey thought that was hilarious especially since the person who asked also happened to be in one of her classes. Jane's favorite course that semester was the study of religious murals in ancient cathedrals.

That summer they spent the bulk of their time at Lacey's home and just a couple of weeks at Jane's parents. They worked at her dad's spa, this time for pay versus treatments. They were saving up with the goal in mind to take a trip, to Europe over the holidays together. They had even planned to continue working part time their junior year to help fund the trip. Jane joked that Lacey just wanted to be on the same continent as Anthony again.

Lacey often replied "Please if even 10 percent of Europeans are as good looking as him I do not want to be tied down, I'll sample them all."

They planned on ringing in the New Year in London, after spending Christmas in Paris and touring Holland. Lacey was really pushing for a day in Amsterdam to try the local coffee house wares. The trip planning was becoming so much fun that they discussed doing the same thing the next year with Australia in mind, seeing as how the weather would be summerlike there that time of year. Or maybe even New Zealand.

Chapter Six

Once back at school to start their junior year they again opted for a dorm over an apartment to still have access to the cafeteria and save funds. Plus, it just worked for them. With all of their prerequisites completed the year before, they sadly did not share any drool worthy professors this year.

Before they knew it, it was holiday break again, holding hands they sat in their seats wanting for the plane to take off. The night before their flight they had again made their annual pilgrimage to their favorite Tacky Light Tour houses. Trip or no trip they could not miss that.

This was Lacey's first trip overseas and Jane's second. Lacey leaned on Jane during their time in France. Jane spoke choppy French but since she had been there so recently they somewhat recreated the trip she had taken with her parents. Lacey had one special request. They had to go to the Moulin Rouge, and it was amazing.

Once they were in London Lacey had all of the details of the hottest spot in town to celebrate New Year's. Otherwise they went to all of the main attractions; Buckingham Palace, the London Eye, and Big Ben. They even managed to get their picture taken in one of those red telephone booths..They also rode around (freezing) on the upper level of a double-decker tour bus. Lastly, New Year's Eve they recreated the Abbey Road album cover with a couple of random cute boys, Lacey sweet talked. The boys had nothing planned that night so the girls now conveniently had dates!

When New Year's came Lacey smooched her Brit and Jane gave her Brit a chaste kiss on the cheek. Their trip was well worth all those hours washing and folding spa towels the summer before. They returned to school ready to take on the rest of their junior year.

Not long after their European vacation Lacey began dating Liam. That was how Jane met Wyatt Huntington III. She had been on a few casual dates throughout college but had mainly kept her head down and focused on her class work. Lacey on the other hand sometimes seemed to be majoring in boys. Lacey, now dating Liam had talked Jane into going on double date with his friend Wyatt.

Wyatt Huntington III was a celebrity of sorts on campus. He resembled Robert Redford in his hay day and all the girls wanted to date him. Lacey had purposefully omitted which Wyatt was the blind date because Jane never would have agreed to come otherwise. She would be far too nervous. As they approached the table Lacey observed Jane's eyes widen in recognition and look around the restaurant for emergency exits. When they sat and ordered, Wyatt was a perfect gentleman and Lacey was thrilled for her friend.

Wyatt was well liked on campus and seemed to be as interested in Jane as she was in him. On their first solo date he took her to a local restaurant just off campus. It was crowded with other college students and many of them seemed to recognize Wyatt and were curious who the pretty brunette was with him. When they were seated Jane nervously began twisting her napkin on her lap. When she realized Wyatt was watching her she flushed.

"Nervous?" he asked.

She nodded.

"Don't be" he was very charming "ever been here before?" he asked.

She shook her head no.

"You should try the risotto, it is wonderful."

When the waiter returned to take their orders he seemed pleased when she did order what he had recommended. Though, she was taken aback by Wyatt's attitude toward the waiter. Her father had always told her that people who mistreated waiters and other clerks were the ones to watch out for. She thought about it but then let it go because he was being so sweet and attentive to her.

After dinner they both went back to Jane's dorm. As they rode the elevator to her floor he pulled her against his body and ran his hands up and down her back. Lacey had plans for the evening so she had thought she would still be out. Lacey wasn't. Wyatt actually seemed pretty annoyed that Lacey was there and left shortly.

Jane sent him a text apologizing, no response. She could not fall asleep that night unable to stop thinking about the evening and stressing. What if she had ruined things and Wyatt would not like her anymore. He was the first guy to have really shown interest in her and she thought he was very attractive. She worried that he could have even thought she was a tease and had lied about Lacey being out.

The next morning she explained her concerns to Lacey. Lacey sat listening with a very perplexed look on her face. When Jane had finished Lacey asked her why she was so stressed out about a guy she's barely gone out with. Jane couldn't describe her attraction to him. Lacey rolled her eyes and told her not to worry.

"You weren't going to sleep with him were you?" Lacey asked surprised.

"I don't know."Jane admitted honestly.

Lacey stared at her open mouthed. Lacey was no virgin but as Jane's best friend knew that Jane was.

"I'm not going to tell you not to do this but I am going to say I think you should get to know Wyatt a bit more before you do" Lacey advised.

Jane could agree with her logic but she also felt that Wyatt was the type of guy that could be bored easily. Besides if they ended up dating seriously what would it matter how long they waited before becoming intimate she thought.

Lacey shook her head at Jane and said "Just use protection darling."

Jane blushed and nodded.

Here she was discussing her possible first time, then she remembered how annoyed Wyatt looked when he left. She figured she wouldn't hear from him again and went on about her day. She was thrilled when she received a text back from him that afternoon. He wrote that he was going to a party that night, and would she want to meet him there.

She replied back right away that she would love to. Wanting tonight to be perfect she asked Lacey if she could raid her closet. Lacey raised her eyebrow at her but otherwise agreed. It was cold outside so Jane ended up wearing a pair of slim jeans tucked into black boots. She picked a pretty emerald top of Lacey's, somewhat low cut. Under it all, she purposely wore her prettiest underwear set just in case. Lacey and Liam were also going to the same party and Jane rode with them.

Chapter Seven

W hen they got there Wyatt was already buzzed sitting in a lazy boy in the living room with a pretty blonde on his lap. Jane was mortified and rushed to a bathroom to compose herself. Lacey followed her after looking pointedly at Liam. When he just shrugged, she threw her hands up and left him standing there. She followed Jane into the bathroom. Jane stood there fanning her face.

"Who is that girl?" she cried "Do you think he saw me?" Lacey did her best to calm her friend down.

Lacey offered to take her back to the dorm and stay with her. Jane was adamant that she wanted to stay because she wasn't sure if he had seen her or not. In that case, Lacey thought, she should have Wyatt come to her because she should under no circumstances acknowledge him or that girl. In fact she recommended Jane talk to any other guy at the party instead. Jane stared at her open mouthed as though she were speaking in tongues.

Lacey huffed and said "Fine I'll introduce you to some people I know."

Jane couldn't help but look over at Wyatt every so often. At one point he caught her eye and waved her over.

Lacey murmured "No way, make him come to you." but Jane was already on her way over to him.

As she approached, he evicted the pretty blonde from his lap. She frowned at Jane and walked away. He motioned for Jane to sit with him.

When she hesitated he said "She was just keeping your seat warm babe.

She shrugged and sat down. Her perch allowed him a clear view down her shirt.

"You look really hot tonight" He murmured drinking her in.

She giggled as he wrapped his arms around her waist and nipped at her neck.

"You coming home with me tonight?" he asked.

She met his gaze and slowly nodded.

He had a couple more drinks, and got a bit handsy with her in front of his friends. Lacey couldn't help but notice and was concerned for her friend. They barely knew each other and he was clearly trashed. When Jane went up to go to the bathroom she went to check on her.

"Everything okay?" She asked.

"Of course" Jane exclaimed happily "He wants me to go home with him."

"So not gonna do that whole 'get to know him better' thing we talked about earlier." Lacey mused.

Jane shook her head.

"My little girl is growing up." Lacey joked. "But seriously" she continued "Be safe and make him take his time. You better tell me all about it tomorrow."

Jane solemnly promised to and they returned to the party.

When Jane got back to Wyatt he said "This party blows, let's get out of here."

He lived a very short walk from where the party was. Once in his apartment Jane looked around. It was really nice in comparison to other college apartments she had seen. There was actual framed art on the walls, and it was very clean. Too clean for a college guy, she wondered if he had a cleaning service.

He took her coat and rested it on the back of a chair near the door. Taking her hand he led her to the living room and sat down in front of her on the sofa. Picking up a remote he turned on a stereo somewhere. The speakers were hooked up to a surround system and the room filled with classic rock. Feeling self conscious still standing, Jane went to sit next to him.

"Uh uh" he said stopping her "take off your clothes." He leaned back and watched her.

She blushed and crossed her arms over her chest.

"Don't be a prude." he said. She uncrossed her arms and went to slip off her boots and socks.

"Do it more sexy." Wyatt demanded.

Isn't talking your clothes off in front of someone already sexy she thought to herself. She continued to remove her boots and while began slightly rocking her hips to the beat of the music she pulled her shirt over head and began unbuttoning her jeans. Once they were unbuttoned he brought his hands up to slide them down her legs. She stood there for a moment in just her bra and underwear. She took a deep breath and unhooked her bra then shrugged it off.

"I thought you had bigger boobs." he said staring at her chest.

She brought her arms up to cover herself. He placed his hands on her hips and brought her a step forward to him and then slowly pulled her underwear down. She stepped out of them and moved one hand to cover herself. He stood up and told her to undress him. She slowly unbuttoned his oxford shirt. Possibly thinking she was taking too long he brushed her hands off and quickly finished undressing.

He stood naked in front of her and taking her hands he said "Make me hard."

She gingerly touched him with her fingertips, unsure of what she was doing. It seemed to be working though. Once he was fully aroused he led her to his bedroom and motioned her to lay down. He quickly took a condom from a box on his bedside table and put it on. He then covered her with his body and pushed deeply into her.

She would have cried out in pain but she bit her lip not wanting ruin it for him. He went on like that for a few minutes at one point sitting back and pulling her legs up and placing them on each of his shoulders to enter her deeper. She moaned in what she hoped he would think pleasure. When he was finished he got up and went into the bathroom to clean up.

Reentering the room he asked "You sleeping here tonight?"

"If you want me to" Jane replied unsure.

"Alright, but you have to leave early because I have to go somewhere tomorrow."

She cringed inwardly "That's okay" she said.

He lay down next to her and pulled the covers over them.

"I'm just going to run to the bathroom."Jane said getting up.

After using the bathroom she splashed cold water on her face and looked in the mirror.

"Be cool" she said to herself and went back to the bedroom.

When she got back into his bed she realized he was already asleep. She hugged herself resolving to be exactly what Wyatt wanted in a girl and he would fall in love with her. She woke to him taking one of her nipples in his mouth, his hand parting her legs and fingers entering her.

"You wet?" he whispered in her ear.

When he mounted her this time it didn't hurt as bad as the previous time. When he finished he went to take a shower. As he dressed he told her he would drop her off at her place on his way out. She went to retrieve her clothes from the living room and quickly dressed. She grabbed a piece of gum from her purse but desperately wished for a toothbrush.

"Was that your first time?" Wyatt asked.

She met his eyes and nodded.

He then said that was what he had assumed because it was clear she didn't know what she was doing. Shame washed over her as she let that sink in. He dropped her off in front of her dorm with no mention of seeing her again.

Chapter Eight

S he felt so stupid and really sore. She really wished she had a bathtub to just soak in. Lacey was asleep when she tip toed in. She grabbed her bath stuff and went to take a shower. She felt dirty and used. After showering and brushing her teeth she threw on sweats and ate a bowl of cereal.

After her cereal she pretended to be sleep. She did not want to tell Lacey what had happened. Eventually she went from pretending to actually sleeping. When she woke up Lacey was not there. It was after noon and since it was Sunday she did not have a class she could just stay in bed all day.

She took a couple of Advil and checked her phone. No message from Wyatt, somehow she wasn't surprised. She began to feel silly that she even thought she had a chance with him. Lacey came back to the dorm an hour later, when she walked in the door Jane's resolve crumbled and she burst out into tears.

"Oh my God Jane! What's wrong?" Lacey exclaimed rushing over to her.

"I am so stupid" Jane sobbed and went on to tell Lacey what happened the night before and this morning.

Lacey was furious and used some very strong language in detailing what she would do to him the next time she saw him. She couldn't stay angry for too long though as it was clear that was not helping Jane. She enveloped Jane into a bear hug and rocked her not unlike a child as she told her everything would be alright.

Jane calmed down and admitted she mainly felt stupid thinking Wyatt might actually have liked her more than anything else.

Lacey was aghast and she asked "After last night why would you even want him to like you? You don't still like him?"

Jane lowered her head.

"Jane!" Lacey exclaimed.

"I don't know what's wrong with me." Jane sniffled.

"Alright, get your butt up. I am not going to let you sit here and pine over that asshole. We're going to get coffee, my treat" Lacey said tugging Jane's arm.

"Uh uh, I am never leaving this room again for as long as I live. In fact" she continued melodramatically "I need to contact my professors to let them know I will complete my courses via correspondence from this day forward."

After a long pause they both burst out laughing.

"Dork, come on, get up. Free coffee" Lacey said laughing.

"How can I be laughing right now?" Jane asked surprised.

"Because, you have now joined the ranks of women everywhere who lost their virginity to a dickhead. You'll live, just like all of us" Lacey replied.

How did she always know the right thing to say? Jane wondered. Either way, she got up pulled on a pair of boots over her sweats, threw on a jacket and they headed out. Once at the coffee shop Jane resolved abstain from boys or relationships for at least the next year. Lacey rolled her eyes at that. They went on to discuss other things. Lacey told her how things were going with Liam. Not well, unfortunately but that actually may now be a positive since he was friends with Wyatt. That was why she was at the dorm last night.

He had annoyed her at the party so she left him there. He had been texted her ever since but she was just ignoring him. Jane wanted to someday have that ability to not care and said so.

"Don't think that I don't care about Liam just because I don't feel like talking to him right now" Lacey said "It's alright that we argue now and then I guess. He just has to respect that I have a right to my opinion. And right now my opinion is he is wrong."

Later that evening Jane's phone rang.

"It's Wyatt!" Jane exclaimed.

"Don't ans.." was all Lacey got out as Jane said

"Hello" answering the call waving her off.

Lacey's jaw dropped as she sat there thinking 'oh no she didn't...'. Jane was all smiles when she hung up. She turned to face Lacey and her smile faltered.

"Wyatt's coming to get me..." she mumbled.

"What happened to abstaining from boys? Plus he was such a tool to you."Lacey offered knowing it would get her nowhere.

"Maybe he's sorry."Jane said.

Lacey huffed, then went on "I love you and you are a big girl so I can't stop you from seeing him. I just want you to know that I don't think he is the right guy for you."

Jane nodded and said "I appreciate your concern, but I

really like him. If this ends up being a mistake, I promise you can tell me you told me so."

Lacey frowned as she watched Jane rush to shower and change. She put on some cute black pants and a red turtle neck. She twisted her still wet hair into a bun and put on some powder and perfume. She checked her clock, threw her toothbrush in her purse hugged Lacey and was out the door.

From that point on Jane and Wyatt were officially an item on campus. Jane adored him and did everything in her power to please him. If he liked a sports team, she rooted for them. If he liked a band, she bought their CD and would learn to love them as well. He was never very affectionate in public. Jane felt the most happiness when he would on occasion hold her hand, when they were out and about. He was very jealous of any male attention Jane got whether actual or only perceived. This confused Jane because surely he knew she only cared for him. To avoid his annoyance on the subject though, she steered clear of guys in general just to be safe.

Chapter Nine

Jane was becoming so wrapped up in his schedule that her own grades were faltering. Granted she was a straight A student and was in no jeopardy of failing any of her courses, she was just turning into more of a C student. To try and curb this, she began sleeping less and working on her assignments when Wyatt was sleeping. She was exhausted but felt it was worth it in the long run. The one thing that she seemed to have less time for, the she missed the most, was sketching.

Wyatt had taken to remarking on the condition of her hands and nails. She, in the past, had always used her fingers to help blend the shades of whatever she was working on. Doing this over time caused a couple of her fingers to have calluses and she used to keep her nails trimmed to the extreme to aid in this. Wyatt thought it looked 'butch' to have such short nails so she started getting her nails done. After a while she became so busy supporting him in all of his activities she stopped drawing outside of class.

Lacey grew to tolerate him because Jane seemed to be

on cloud nine but she never liked him. When Wyatt began ordering for Jane at restaurants she would gush "Isn't it so sweet, he knows exactly what I like." Lacey thought it cute until when eating out with them she noticed Wyatt order stuff she knew Jane disliked. She raised an eyebrow at Jane in a silent question and Jane just shrugged in response.

She called Jane out on the ordering thing once and her response was "that Wyatt was helping her improve her palate." She could not look Lacey in eyes when she said it. Lacey didn't want her disliking Wyatt to come between them so for once in her life she held her tongue. Part of her felt if she said anything Jane would just become defensive and it would start an argument.

Jane was almost under a spell, and for her Wyatt could do no wrong. When he corrected her or urged her, in a path she would not have normally taken she truly felt it was because he was superior to her. She thought that since there were so many girls pining to date him, and that it was up to her to fit his mold of an ideal girlfriend. Yes, sometimes she would second guess him but she mostly keep those as internal questions.

The feeling of walking into a room and suddenly being important was something new to Jane. Girls envied her and other boys now also wanted to date her. As much as it drove Wyatt crazy, although she did her best to avoid it, his interest in her seemed to increase other's as well. Even if a classmate said hello to Jane when they were out he would give her a look of almost warning and she would excuse herself to avoid any additional attention.

His family was well known around town. His father was some elected official at the capital. Also, for the first time in her life, Jane's mother had nothing to criticize her for. After a fancy formal dinner with Wyatt and his family, Jane could do no wrong. Her father was less impressed but was, if not strong, at least silent on the matter.

It was true Jane could agree that Wyatt was a bit bossy, but she could pardon that in him because he was on a clear life path and needed a supportive partner. He knew more about life than she did and she appreciated the encouragement he gave her to be a person ideal enough to be with him. She began watching her weight and traded her normal jeans and t-shirt look for a reflection of her childhood wardrobe of knee length skirts with the addition of heels.

That was the tricky part there was a fine line between looking polished and looking sexy. Wyatt wanted her to be or look sexy only for him behind closed doors. Otherwise he almost wanted her to look dowdy in public. One time, when they were out with some of his friends, she was wearing a skirt a bit shorter than normal. It was very pretty and she hoped Wyatt would be happy with how nice she looked.

Instead while his friends were preoccupied with something, he hissed in her ear "I take you out with my friends and you dress like a cheap whore."

She must have look so visibly stunned because one of his friends asked if she was alright. Seeing Wyatt glare at them she excused herself saying she was feeling ill. She could not see how Wyatt had thought her skirt was trashy but threw it away anyway as soon as she got home.

When Lacey saw it in the trash she asked Jane about it.

"I just don't like it anymore" she said.

Unable to bite her tongue in time Lacey returned "Or somebody else didn't like it."

Jane looked down and retreated to her side of the room. Lacey kicked herself for saying anything. She missed her best friend. The distance between them grew quickly at that point.

After that Jane began spending more of her time at Wyatt's apartment. His posh two bedroom apartment was just off campus. When she first began spending the night, they would just stay in all the time with the exception of classes and his family events. She still had her dorm room with Lacey and would run there from time to time to pick up more clothes.

When Lacey ran into her at school a few weeks later she did a double take. Jane had always been slim, now she looked skinny to a level that had to be unhealthy.

"Jane!" Lacey called out.

Jane saw her and turned and walked in another direction.

Lacey ran her down. "Avoiding me now?" she asked furious.

"I'm not avoiding you" Jane lied.

But she was and that was something she was not even able to accept herself. She knew Wyatt was not crazy about Lacey and thought she was a bad influence. If she didn't see Lacey she could talk herself into the idea that she was not doing it on purpose, that they were both just busy. She missed her friend but it was almost as if a line had been drawn in her mind. On one side she had Lacey and the other Wyatt. She had to do everything in her power to keep Wyatt so there was nothing else she could do.

"Darling" Wyatt oozed walking up to Jane and putting his arm around her shoulders with her back to him.

"Is she bothering you dear?" He asked eyes locked on Lacey's.

"No, Wyatt. Lacey was just saying hello."

"Fine, well say goodbye Jane we have somewhere to be."

Jane raised her eyes to Lacey and did her best to say how she felt through her eyes. "Sorry Lace, I have to run."

She turned in Wyatt's grasp so that now she was beside him instead of in front and they made their way. A few yards away Jane turned her head back to look at Lacey and smile. Wyatt with his arm still around her shoulders noticed the direction of her glance and said something in her ear. She instantly turned forward and did not look back again.

Lacey walked to a bench nearby and sat trying to wrap her brain around what had just happened. She got an email later that week from Jane letting her know she would officially be moving out of the dorm they shared and into Wyatt's apartment. Jane sent an email instead of calling or talking to Lacey in person because she wasn't sure if she could actually go through with it.

Wyatt's place did not feel like home as her dorm with Lacey had been. It was cold, also even though she had moved in with the exception of her clothes in the closet and dresser and stuff in the bathroom, there was nothing there that was hers. She felt as though she were a guest as Wyatt was very picky about his things. A maid did come weekly to change the sheets and do his laundry, in addition to cleaning the apartment. Between her visits Jane did her best to keep everything just so. Wyatt would get annoyed if he turned on the TV and it was tuned to one of her channels. He also railed at her if she shed anywhere. She could understand why a random strand of hair would bother him so much. She considered cutting her hair but knew he preferred it long.

Her clothes hung on her, she could see she had lost weight. She was just under so much stress with school and trying to keep Wyatt happy. When he mentioned to her, off hand, that they would be spending the summer with his parents at their beach house she felt even more stressed. She wished she had time to sketch or paint but Wyatt did not like her supplies at his place. She could only work at the studio on campus, but he didn't like her working there because it was a communal space. So unless she was at her parent's house, she basically didn't pursue it.

One night they were going to a party at the home of one of Wyatt's fraternity buddies. It was warm out so Jane wore an embellished tank and a simple skirt. In the car Wyatt seemed annoyed about something so Jane asked if everything was alright. He shrugged in response not answering.

When they got there Wyatt walked ahead of her, leaving her to walk in alone. Jane hated walking in a parties or clubs or just about any situation alone. She felt eyes on her as she entered the house. The place was crowded and she did not recognize anyone she knew in the front room. She made her way through the house towards the kitchen hoping Wyatt would be there getting a drink. He wasn't.

Next she went through the back door to the patio, still looking for Wyatt. He was there, already doing tequila shots with some sorority girls. She stood there as if she had grown roots watching him lick salt off of the neck of a pretty red head. He caught her eye and smirked at her. What an asshole she thought to herself. He always acted like this when he was in a rotten mood about something. It was like he wanted to see just how far he could push her.

Sad thing was Jane knew she would not do anything about it. She felt her face flush and was paranoid that people were staring at her, maybe even feeling sorry for her. Pivoting on her heels she went back inside and to the bathroom to take a few deep breathes. She tried to decide what to do next. 'Go back outside and watch him flirt with everyone, no thank you' she thought to herself. Part of her just wanted to walk back to his place. That would serve him right, but she knew she never would. She was too scared it might give him a reason to break up with her.

She jumped as someone knocked on the door. Not leaving or going back to the backyard she settled on sitting by herself in an armchair in the corner of the living room. A few people offered her drinks and tried to make small talk. She just nodded and smiled politely till they left. After a bit Wyatt came looking for her and seemed to be in a better mood. She accepted his outstretched hand and he pulled her into a deep embrace. Though, it was not the kind of kiss she felt comfortable having in a crowded room full of strangers.

She gently pushed at him embarrassed "Wyatt, people are watching."

He released her and took a step away from her. "You are such a prude" he said loudly and then turned and walked off.

She looked down, pulling her lips between her teeth, sucking air in through her nose. When she looked up she caught the sympathetic eyes of a few girls. One had her hand over her mouth in a 'oh no he didn't' stance. Jane could feel tears threatening and refused to show any emotion she calmly walked back towards the bathroom repeating 'you do not deserve this' over and over in her mind until she was able to shut the door behind her.

Appraising herself in the mirror she thought about how Wyatt must have felt to come and kiss her in front of all of those people and then have her push him away. He wasn't the jerk, she was. She reapplied her lip gloss and fluffed her hair. He was back out on the patio and she quietly went to go stand with him. He glanced at her with a look that said 'thought you would be back'. He pulled her to his side one hand firmly planted on her ass. Later she followed him to one of the upstairs bedrooms despite his wolfish grin and the catcalls of his friends following after them.

It embarrassed her that people would know what they were doing up there and Wyatt knew it. She went along with it any ways to make up for upsetting him earlier. They eventually left the party she drove since Wyatt drank so much. After brushing her teeth she was relieved to see he had already passed out. It made her uncomfortable to admit how pleased she was to not have to be intimate with him again that night.

Chapter Ten

Summer break was quickly approaching and after that their senior year. Wyatt took Jane to his family's summer home at the beach. She drove herself down in her new car, it used to be her mother's but was now hers, since her mom got a new one. It was a silver four door sedan. Windows down, she cruised down the highway. She let her mind wonder and her thoughts drifted to Lacey. She wondered what Lacey would be doing over the summer break. Would Lacey stay in town or would she go back home to Iowa? When she finally arrived she was thrilled to see they were beach front.

Being able to hear the rhythmic beat of the waves from the driveway made Jane really want to check out the view from off the decks the pastel home boasted. Jane knocked on the door suitcase in hand. Wyatt met her and showed her to the room they would be sharing. He, then gave her a quick tour, and took her up to see his parents who were having a drink on an upper deck.

It was the first opportunity Jane had to really see his family dynamic. It was not healthy. His father was a well documented adulterer. His mother the picture of the stead-fast loyal wife by his side, never showing emotion thanks to her regularly scheduled Botox appointments. She was also an obsessive control freak, Jane wondered to herself it this is was who Wyatt had gotten it from. She fixated on every-thing else around her to clearly avoid the issues of her husband. Wyatt who was their only child was her pride and joy and could do no wrong.

It was clear she had political aspirations for him. It was also clear she did not share Wyatt's view that Jane was a suitable companion for his future. In her mind, since Jane's family did not have any true wealth or power to aid her son, she was just temporary. His mother seems to also believe that Jane was inviting the attention of her husband. Jane felt so unsure of how she was supposed to behave.

She was only trying to be polite, she just wanted them to like her. It was discouraging to realize, she did not think they would like her no matter what she did. She could also see Wyatt was becoming annoyed that she was not getting on with his parents. What was meant to be a relaxing vaca-tion at the beach with her boyfriend, was anything but. Most days were spent by the pool or on the beach. Jane had stocked up on conservative one piece bathing suits. She looked as though she had stepped out of a movie from the 50's.

There was a second floor deck off the den that over-looked the pool and the beach. In the mornings they would all eat breakfast there. After breakfast Wyatt, and some-times his mother, would take Jane out around town. There were many quaint touristy shops that offered a multitude of souvenirs for the vacationers. Jane picked up a couple of things for her parents and Lacey. They would have lunch out, mainly seafood at local restaurants. Once back at the house, they would rest by the pool or beach until dinner.

She felt as though she was making a very good impression. Wyatt's dad was mainly absent, constantly taking calls for work and working in his office. Wyatt's mother was still cool to her but she hoped over time that maybe, just maybe she could grow to like her. They had a chef on hire preparing the main supper meals. Weather depending, they would eat on the 3rd floor deck with one of the best ocean views.

The scenery was so beautiful Jane would sit on the deck and sketch. Pad and pencil free hands that she hoped to translate to oil or water color once back at home. She was drawing a seagull perched on a post with the beach and waves behind. Wyatt's mother approached her once while she was sketching and mustered a

"Not bad" when she saw Jane's drawing. Jane was elated, that was the nicest thing his mother had said to her all summer. She thanked her and smiled brightly. "It's nice to have a hobby" Wyatt's mother said walking away. Considering this was Jane' work that comment was crushing. She put her supplies away and went to find Wyatt.

It especially hurt because she had not taken the time to draw, in so long. Here she thought being on vacation, she could try to pick it back up again. Sure her nails were longer now but she thought it was still a fair effort. Maybe it was time for her to hang it up altogether.

She tried to stay close to Wyatt most of the time in an attempt to avoid any uncomfortable situations. One morning, when she woke up he had gone to the store for his mother. She contemplated staying in their room till he returned. Then she heard his mother say "Is that girl going to sleep all day?" At that Jane decided maybe a solitary stroll on the beach would be a good plan.

She put on her suit and a wrap and headed out the door. His parents were eating breakfast on the upstairs deck. She waved to them as she headed towards the beach. She laid down with a book and lost track of time. Other beach goers had came and set up all around her.

A game of beach volleyball began some yards from her. A couple of young men approached her with an invitation to play. She waved them off and resumed her book. One inquired as to the title of her book. She silently tilted the book so the cover was visible then again returned to reading. Seeing she was not interested they moved on.

Jane checked her watch and realizing it was past lunchtime gathered her things and returned to the house. Wyatt was seated on the same porch his parents had breakfasted earlier. She waved to him and in response he did nothing. Jane felt her heart start thumping. Was he angry at her? she wondered. She hurried inside and put her things in their room.

As she turned to leave the room she was startled by him, he was standing in the doorway leaned up against the frame.

"I was just coming up" she said walking towards him.

"We all saw you" he replied coolly.

"What?" she asked.

"You know what" he said raising his voice.

"Wyatt I have no idea what you are talking about" she returned.

"Do you think I'm stupid?" he yelled his face becoming red. "I invite you to my parent's home, for what? For you to dress like a slut and go hit on men at the beach."

"Wyatt I didn't, I was just reading..."

He cut her off "I watched you"

"But Wyatt.." she stammered.

"In front of my parents. My mom told me you were trash and I didn't believe her. Thanks for showing me I was wrong. Get your shit and get out of my house."

He left the room. She stood there stunned then slowly collected her things, loaded her suitcase into her car and drove away. She only made it one block before she dissolved into tears and had to pull over. She sat there for an hour sobbing before she could compose herself enough to drive. She was humiliated. She played the scene on the beach then Wyatt's reaction over and over in her head. What could she have done differently? She had not even spoken to those men. She cringed at the thought that Wyatt's mother had called her trash.

Chapter Eleven

She did not trust her voice so while pumping gas she sent a text to her mom letting her know she was heading home. Having to go home unexpectedly to her parents with no explanation of why she left or why Wyatt was not with her was a nightmare. Her mother peppered her with questions that she had no answers for. She went to her room without eating and cried herself to sleep. The next day her mother started in on her again. Jane gave up and called Lacey hoping she was still in town.

Lacey invited her to the apartment downtown she was renting over the summer. Once Jane got there she instantly felt a sense of peace. It was a soft place to fall considering to current status of her heart. Which was officially broken. It was in a converted row house and had rich antique wood floors, doors and trim.

Lacey's initial reaction to Jane calling her was to blow her off, but after hearing the desperation of her voice she didn't want to abandon her. Lacey realized that regardless of Jane's behavior towards the end of the semester, what type of friend would Lacey be if she wasn't willing and ready to be there for Jane when she needed her most? The first day they were together they behaved like magnets with their polarities reversed. They stayed on opposite sides of her apartment and observed each other, each one not ready to began the conversation.

Finally Lacey unable to contain herself any longer said "So what's the deal with you and Wyatt?"

Jane put her head in her hands. She was miserable without him, she could not contemplate functioning with the hole his disappearance left in her.

"I just don't know" was all she could muster.

Lacey, unable to ignore the pain her friend was obviously in, came to wrap her arms around her. Jane feeling the unconditional support of her friend just unloaded and wept. Lacey stayed there rubbing her back and telling her it would be alright until Jane got most of it out. As Jane sat sniffling on the sofa, Lacey force fed her crackers, bottled water and had a never ending supply of tissue. The two ended up passing out on the sofa sometime after 3am. The next day Lacey convinced Jane a shower would be in her best interest.

There is a psychological uplifting feeling cleanliness will do to a soul. Jane felt mentally exhausted though. She had played the beach trip over and over in her mind and could not think of anything she could have done differently. She felt very awkwardly thankful that Lacey was still a soft place to land even though she had pushed her away in the last year. She felt a level of guilt in even having to ask. Jane just couldn't face her mother's questions and had nowhere else to go.

Even though Lacey was exactly what she needed right now, it bothered Jane that she wasn't asking more questions. It made her feel like in all of the time they were friends this was proof that Lacey was a better friend to her than she was in return. That was a bitter thought to swallow. It also made her if only momentarily, angry at Wyatt who was a main source of her separation from Lacey.

Lacey got her eating and somewhat talking by lunch time. She briefly explained the interactions with Wyatt's family at the beach. Lacey was dumbstruck. How was she going to be able to reach Jane when Jane could not even acknowledge how dysfunctional that family unit was. Lacey could not understand how Jane was certain she had done something wrong.

In an effort to not upset Jane further or quite frankly lose it, Lacey brought up their approaching senior year for discussion. There was life after this Jane lamented. Lacey was not used to being the least dramatic friend in the room, this really worrying her. She even contemplated recommending that Jane speak to a professional but she didn't want to offend her.

Lacey made spaghetti and put a comedy on. She watched Jane eating like a hawk. Thankfully there seem to be some sign of her appetite returning. Afterward she set up the sofa for Jane to sleep on and went to bed. She woke to Jane sobbing, just before midnight. Shaking off sleep she went to her. Jane was a blubbering mess just beside herself over the loss of Wyatt.

Jane was ashamed that she had woken Lacey up. She just could not control the pain she was feeling. It seemed as when she had felt as though she had reached a bottom and was coming to terms with what was going on that it would drop out from under her again and she would be crashing through space fearfully awaited the impact of a new deeper bottom. Her first bottom was the fear of what other people would think.

Obviously Wyatt was perfect, so everyone would think it was her fault, and that she had done something. She

wondered if she should move her things out of their apartment. She wanted to get everything out before he was back
in town but also leave it in the hopes he would have to
contact her to arrange some sort of pick up. Then the
shame of not having her mother feel as proud as she had
been. Today it was the reeling terror of not being sure
what to do with herself. Three days ago she had an identity
and a future all laid out for herself. She truly believed she
would be the future Mrs. Wyatt Huntington III.

Now she was just Jane Martin with no plan and no
future. That was scary. Sometime after three, they finally
drifted back to sleep on the couch. When Lacey woke up
the next morning she wondered to herself if this was not
unlike waking up each night with a newborn. She suddenly
felt much more empathy to any new parent she had ever
met because she was exhausted and praying for a full night
of sleep tonight.

Jane was very subdued that morning and felt so dehy-
drated she didn't think she could cry, even if she wanted to,
at that moment. Lacey brought her a bowl of fruit loops
and it struck Jane at that moment how much she actually
missed Fruit Loops. She recalled reaching for a box while
out shopping with Wyatt and he had made fun of her
questioning her opinion and prompted her to choose a
sensible no flavor wheat cereal instead. She hated that
cereal, it tasted like cardboard. But Jane remembered at
that moment that Lacey had never really liked Fruit Loops,
she was more of a Cocoa Puffs girl.

"Fruit Loops?" Jane asked.

"They grew on me" was all Lacey would say.

She savored her Fruit Loops and apologized to Lacey
for waking her up again. Lacey said that whether she liked
it or not they were venturing out today. Jane pouted and
Lacey pointedly ignored her.

"Jane it is a beautiful day out and this complex has a pool, so grab a book and borrow my frumpiest bathing suit and let's go." Lacey had an extensive swim wear collection so Jane was able to borrow simple black one piece while Lacey opted for a fire engine red bikini.

Even though Jane had plenty of suits they were all at her parent's house. She had not thought to bring one when Lacey invited her over. It was early so the pool area was almost empty, but it was going to be a very hot day out so the calm was not going to last long. They selected a couple of lounges with a good early sun angle. After applying sunscreen Lacey flipped through a magazine while Jane continued the book she had started at the beach. There was still sand in the binding. It made it hard not to obsess about the beach when it seems to almost be following her.

She wondered how Wyatt was doing, was he missing her? Did he even care? That last question was too painful to consider. She got up after a while and went to put her feet in the water to cool off. Lacey got up and came to join her.

"Yikes it's hot out" she said "My feet were burning just walking over here."

Jane smiled in response and then said "Lacey I really appreciate you being there for me."

At the threat of another on slot of eminent tears Lacey interrupted "No need to say anything else, I got you babe."

Jane wiped her eyes and leaned her head on Lacey's shoulder. After a few moments she and Lacey got back up and went to lay back down. Lacey fussed around trying to get comfortable and then once noticing a group of attractive guys over by the vending machine was suddenly very thirsty and in immediate need of the bottle of water. Jane watched her envious, where did that confidence come from?

She never seemed to care if a guy liked her or not (and they always did). Can that be learned? How do you just not care what other people think? Lacey was heading back over.

"So two of those guys over there asked about you" she said sitting down.

"Liar" Jane said turning a page in her book.

"I would never lie to you" Lacey huffed. The idea of any guy other than Wyatt was something Jane was not ready to accept at this point.

Lacey went on "I heard somewhere the best way to get over one man is to get under another" winking.

Jane scrunched her nose at her and got up again to put her feet in the water. She glanced over at the group Lacey had referred to and was surprised to see a couple of them wave at her. She smiled back thinking could it really be that easy? No, she was heartbroken there would be no one else for her ever. She would spend the rest of her days as an old maid. Maybe even adopt a few cats.

She was roused from her daydream by a young man swimming over to where she sat. She contemplated jumping up and running back to her lounge, but he was already too close to her for her to get away in time.

"Hello" he began leaning against the side of the pool.

"Hi" Jane returned.

"I'm Caleb" he said putting a hand out.

"Nice to meet you, I'm Jane."

They spoke for a couple of minutes and all Jane could think was he seemed nice but he had nothing on Wyatt. He asked what she and Lacey were doing later and mentioned that he and his friends were having a get barbeque, if they would like to come. Jane told him she would check with Lacey and let him know. With that he swam back over to his friends and Jane got up to go lay back down.

"Hey I saw that guy talking to you" Lacey said as she opened her book "what'd he want?"

"We have been invited to something they are having tonight" Jane replied.

"Do you want to go?" Lacey inquired excitedly.

Jane gave her a look like what do you think.

Lacey shrugged "Come on, I think it would be good for you."

"I'll think about it" was the best Jane could do. "Can we please go inside now? I think I might melt." Jane moaned.

"Fine, but first let me go find out a little bit more about this shin-dig" Lacey said sashaying back over to the guys.

Jane packed her stuff up and Lacey's then walked over and waited for her, by the exit. Lacey seeing her headed over and gave her the details on the way back up to her apartment. Jane really wasn't interested in going but could acknowledge staying in and obsessing about what went wrong would not assist her in moving on. She didn't want to admit to Lacey that she did not want to move on. She was at least able to recognize how desperate or sad that made her appear. Lacey had absolutely seen her at her worst but even then Jane was too embarrassed to say that out loud.

Lacey and Jane took turns showering and then shared a bag salad with roasted chicken morsels for lunch. After that Lacey took a nap feeling very drained from the sun. Jane taking advantage of time where she was not being watched, went to check her email. She was secretly hoping to have some sort of communication from Wyatt. Unfortunately the only new email was from her mother. It mentioned trying to get a hold of her via cell phone multiple times.

It made Jane realize she had not even seen her phone

since she got to Lacey's. She tore through her bags and it was nowhere to been found. She raced out of the apartment down to her car and when she opened the driver side car she spied her phone in the door well. When she went to check it she groaned realizing it was dead. Shutting her door and beeping her car she raced back up to Lacey's apartment and attached her phone to its charger.

It was so drained it would not even turn on. It just gave her a message that once there was enough of a charge it would automatically turn on. She sat on the sofa switching off from watching Lacey's bedroom door to see if she was awake to checking her phone to see if it had turned on yet. She remembered a saying about a watched pot will never boil so she went back to the computer to finish reading the email her mother had written.

It went on to say that Wyatt had been trying to reach her and had actually even called her parents trying to track her down. Her mother was dumbstruck that Jane would treat Wyatt this way, as he was trying to fix whatever had happened at the beach. Jane was in agony, her phone was still charging and now knowing that Wyatt was trying to get to her and she was being unavailable to him killed her inside.

He would never believe that her phone was in her car this whole time. He might not forgive her now that he had to think she was ignoring him. Her manic pacing must have woken Lacey up because she was now coming out of her room rubbing her eyes saying

"What is all this noise?" She was struck by the look of sheer distress on Jane's face. "Jane what's wrong?" she asked concerned.

Jane pointed to the email from her mother still up and open on the computer. Reading it Lacey felt her shoulders sag. So Wyatt was trying to get Jane back she thought mentally preparing herself for her friend to once again be removed from her.

"Where was your phone?" she asked.

"In my car" Jane replied "it is charging right now but was so dead that it still will not turn on."

"Well…" Lacey began "How do you feel about what happened with Wyatt?"

Jane furrowed her brows in confusion didn't Lacey understand this was the solution to all of her problems. "What do you mean?" She answered.

"Are you sure you and Wyatt are right for each other?" there she said it out loud Lacey thought cringing as Jane stared at her open mouthed.

"That is the craziest thing I have ever heard, of course we are right for each other."

"I mean are YOU really happy with Wyatt?" Lacey went on.

"I've only been unhappy right now without him" Jane cried.

"Are you going to ditch me again if you get back together?"

Jane exhaled she could not deny that she had absolutely chosen Wyatt in her life over Lacey. But, doesn't that happen with a lot of couples? You start dating someone seriously and have different interests as a couple than you once had as a single person. Maybe it was just inevitable that she and Lacey would out grow each other. However she could not deny that when every other person in her life had failed her, it was Lacey that she ran to.

The long silence was enough for Lacey

"Forget about it, do what you want." She muttered.

"Wait!" Jane replied "I don't know how it will work but I can tell you one thing. If Wyatt and I do get back together I will not allow our friendship to be affected like I did before. I promise. Besides Wyatt probably will not want anything to do with me, he must think I am ignoring him."

Hopeful Lacey asked "You don't think he would believe you didn't have your phone on you?"

"I don't know" Jane said still looking at her phone miserably.

"Well if you do get back together, what needs to change so that a repeat of whatever happened at the beach doesn't just happen again?" Lacey asked.

She had a point Jane thought, she did love Wyatt but had no such attachment to his parents. Plus they had all actually considered she had been making advances to random people on the beach. How could he ever think that? And, if she could not trust him what hope would they even have in getting married.

She still had not told Lacey everything that had happened down at the beach house, besides if she told her now it would possibly poison her opinion of Wyatt or his family. She decided to wait to see what Wyatt had said, if anything, once her phone was charged. Her phone chirped with life as it turned itself on. She watched it go through all of the startup functions. Leaving it still plugged in, she checked her voicemail first. Multiple messages. The first was from her mother, delete she already knew what her mother wanted.

The next one was from Wyatt and he had called on the day she had arrived at Lacey's. He had said that he was upset at the way they had left things and he felt he had acted rashly in asking her to leave and to call him. The next message was from Wyatt again about 4 hours after the first message. He had reiterated wanting her to call and had even apologized this time.

The next message was also from Wyatt a day after his first 2 messages. He seemed to be becoming put off that she had not called back, yet still seemed apologetic, and asked her to call. The tone of the next call was of a marked difference to the others. It was more of a, who did she think she was to not have called back by now. Oh no. The next message was from her mother half concerned for her because they had no clue where she was, half letting her know Wyatt had called and she would not be the girl she had raised if she did not call that nice young man back pronto.

That was the last message. Next Jane went to check her text messages. There were a bunch and all from Wyatt and none providing any new information. And worse there were no messages following his last voicemail. She cringed and dialed his number. He answered on the second ring. She went on to explain where she was and how she had not had her phone.

Chapter Twelve

Lacey had walking into the kitchen to get a drink and observed the tension in Jane's voice hearing the hope that Wyatt would forgive her. She shook her head thinking how backwards this situation was. He was the one in the wrong, no one in their right mind who knew Jane could believe she could have done what he accused her of. Now her beautiful brilliant friend was doing everything in her power to reestablish a relationship with someone who seemed hell bent on her becoming a Stepford wife.

Wyatt was able with little effort or admittance of wrongdoing, get Jane back. He told her that upon further mediation of events at the beach he was willing to believe her version of events. Jane was so relieved that everything could go back to normal that she accepted whatever he said. Lacey sat there shaking her head at their conversation. How do you convince someone the man of her dreams did not deserve her.

Time moved on, and the only true marked difference between the Jane and Wyatt after the brief break up versus the couple prior was Lacey. Jane was not going to lose her friend this time. Wyatt sensing this alteration in Jane didn't push it. Jane also did not move in with Wyatt their senior year which surprised everyone. She never wanted to feel like she didn't have her own place again. She and Lacey rented an apartment in a historic row house.

Their apartment was a 2 bedroom, 3 floor walk up with no elevator so there was a built in workout, just coming home each day, they joked. The bathroom had a beautiful claw foot tub and separate shower. This was the first place the girls had where they had actual bedrooms in addition to the living area, plus a full kitchen versus the dorm fridge microwave set up they were used to.

As Wyatt grew to learn to tolerate Lacey she again learned to deal with him. Especially now that they had their own bedrooms as now, from time to time, he would spend the night at their place. With him in the picture there was no talk this year of planning or taking a New Year's trip. Which seemed to work out in the long run, as they were all very busy with their classes, being their senior year.

Wyatt had been applying to Graduate schools across the country. He was going to be an Engineer. He and Jane had multiple conversations as to which program would work best for both of them. Jane was not intending on going to graduate school but was looking into future employment /intern opportunities in the locations Wyatt was applying.

Lacey was participating in multiple local productions and was very busy. Wyatt and Jane also were also very publicly visible for a current campaign, as his father was seeking a higher office. His name was even being brought up as a possible Vice President running mate in the next general election. Jane's next step in her ongoing transformation to Stepford, as Lacey sometimes called it, was significant.

She had regular hair and nail appointments. The majority of her clothes and accessories were designer labels. Wyatt was even hinting at buying her a BMW for her birthday, even though she already had a nice Audi, but since it was a hand me down from her mother, in his eyes, it was not new enough. She was his perfect accessory to any formal dinner or function.

For Jane, the second go at her relationship with Wyatt, was less stressful than the first. She had Lacey and her own space to work in. Whatever changes he wanted in her had already mainly happened. She knew what to wear and how she was expected to handle herself. Wyatt was even growing complimentary towards her. She felt as though she had made it through the difficult parts and they were now on course for the long term.

As the Holiday's approached Wyatt and Jane's families were going to celebrate together at the Huntington's home in the mountains. Their mothers were inseparable as Mrs. Huntington enjoyed being fawned over. Their fathers were not as close. Mr. Huntington was busy with work and Mr. Martin just didn't like him. He was polite of course, just distant, and spent most of the trip by the fireplace with a book.

Chapter Thirteen

W yatt snowboarded while Jane tried her hand at skiing. She had hoped he would teach her, but he did not want to. She ended up in 'Snow School' with a large group of elementary school students. She caught Wyatt laughing each time he passed their group. That compelled her to try even harder to be successful at this. When they were released from the school, she managed to make a couple of passes without falling.

She seemed to be most afraid of getting on and off the chair lift. She had visions of face planting in front of the line of people behind her. As she queued up Wyatt took the spot next to her.

"Looking good out there" he said sounding amazed "Never took you for the outdoor type."

She blushed under the praise.

"Wanna see if you can keep up with me down the trail?" he asked.

She shook her head no. He had been snowboarding for years.

"Come on, you can do it" he assured her.

It wasn't so bad at first, either he was taking it easy on her or she was better then she had thought. Wyatt competitive by nature picked up speed and not wanting to race Jane pulled back. When she finally caught up to him, he had wiped out near the base of the trail. He seemed to be in pain and was holding his arm. She rushed over to him and he glared at her.

"Are you hurt?" she called out.

"Clearly" he replied curtly.

"What can I do?" she asked stepping out of her skis.

He had her carry their gear as they made their way to the first aid office. Along the way he was stressing certain his arm was broken. When they got there they were seen immediately. The office, being attached to such a swanky resort, luckily had mobile xray equipment on hand. It was not a break but a sprain. They set Wyatt up with some painkillers and a sling and told him to follow up with his primary physician, once he got home.

Jane was relieved and arranged with the resort staff that their gear be taken back to the Huntington's home. They were within walking distance, so they headed home. Along the way Wyatt blamed Jane for his fall. He said once he got towards the bottom of the trail, he realized she was no longer with him and turned back to look for her when he fell. Jane apologized profusely explaining she was just too slow to keep up with him.

His mother met them at the door. The Lodge had called to make her aware of his fall. He told his mother it was Jane's fault he fell. If her eyes could shoot daggers Jane would be dead. Jane started to explain herself but his mother abruptly raised her hand stopping her. Jane stood there open mouthed as his mother walked with him up the stairs.

She pulled off her boots then followed them. Upstairs

their mothers were cooing over him and again he said it was Jane's fault that he fell. Her father unable to keep his mouth shut said

"I'm not sure if I understand what you are saying young man. Was Jane anywhere near you when you fell?"

"No, as I said, I was looking for her when I fell" Wyatt huffed.

"Well, as I see it, unless she pushed you down or tripped you it's your own fault you fell."

You could have heard a pin drop as every eye in the room was on Jane's father. Silently she agreed with him but knowing Wyatt would not like it, she said

"But, Daddy, I really should have let Wyatt know that I couldn't keep up."

That seemed to placate everyone for the time being. After dinner Jane's father quietly pulled her aside to give her his opinion whether she liked it or not. He made it clear that any man, who needed to blame something as simple as a loss of balance on his partner, would not be likely to accept responsibility for other actions as well.

Seeing the concern in her father's eyes made Jane feel awful. He just couldn't understand this was how Wyatt was and she was okay with it. She wished she could say something to make him feel better but there was nothing. She could tell he paid additional attention to Wyatt from that moment on. She could feel Wyatt sensed it to and saw that he avoided her father. It also made her wish she was with Lacey instead going to see the houses from the Tacky Light Tour. She was really sad that they had missed that this year.

The rest of the vacation went smoothly and they were back at school. Being the last semester of their senior year they all had their heads down as they focused on class work. Finals would be there before they knew it. Wyatt had already been receiving some notifications of acceptance for Graduate school. They were all in the happy positions of knowing they were passing. What was most stressful at the time was the decisions they had to make once they were outside of the comfort zone of University.

Wyatt's decision was mainly which school to attend. Lacey was contemplating moving to New York to try to make it on Broadway. Jane was just waiting for Wyatt to decide where he was going to, so she could plan her move as well. All she could do in the mean time was wait.

Wyatt was increasingly distant. Jane did her best to try to engage him but she just could not figure it out. She finally gave up and just hoped he was stressing over which school to pick. By finals, she wasn't really speaking to either Wyatt or Lacey. They were all ships just passing each other on different paths. Wyatt and Jane both had class organized late night cram fests. Lacey studied solo and since a portion of her final was performance, did her best to rest her body and voice.

Once finals were all over there was a feeling euphoria over all of them. Wyatt seemed back to his old self so Jane was relived. Packing for all began in earnest. Wyatt had selected a very Prestigious Grad school in Chicago. Jane was going to spend the summer with her folks, before moving out there to be with him. She was doing her best to have an internship, at a museum set up before graduation.

Lacey had been cast as a lead in a local production of "Arsenic and Old Lace" so she had put off any consideration of moving until it's run was complete. Jane, reliving their first summer together, helped out with the set creation, until Wyatt voiced his concern at her being around so many artsy types. Lacey tried talking Jane into staying with her over the summer but, since Jane knew Wyatt wouldn't like that, she declined. Besides it's not like they weren't going to hang out, with her parent's house being so close.

Graduation Day was here. Each walked across the stage under the proud eyes of their parents. Wyatt's parents were hosting a big party in his honor. Jane was of course attending and Lacey were also invited. Jane had a feeling it was going to be a big night. Her mother had got it into her head that Wyatt would propose to her that night. She took extra care in getting ready for the party wanting to look her best.

When they arrived, Jane went to find Wyatt but couldn't. His mother was no help either saying that she didn't know where he was, which was unlikely. Giving up, she found Lacey and hung out with her until she saw him. Their house had one of those sweeping entry staircases with an expanse at the top of the stair. He was standing up there with his mother, in what appeared to be a tense conversation. Jane stayed where she was, not wanting to march into the middle of something.

Most of the party goers mingled, sipping champagne and enjoying trays of h'orderves that were being circulated, when Mr. Huntington gave a short speech. He thanked everyone for coming and praised his son on graduating, mentioning the school he would be going on to in the fall. Once he was finished, Wyatt said a few words. Mostly repeating what his father had just said. Towards the end of his speech Jane held her breath hoping that her mother was right. She was not. Wyatt's speech came to an end, with no proposal.

Hopes dashed she politely mingled until her paths finally crossed with Wyatt's. He asked her if he could speak to her privately, and all at once she was sure he was going to ask her to marry him. They went into his father's first floor office and he shut the door. His breath smelled of scotch and he molded his hands to her. Not speaking he turned her around and bent her over his father's desk.

Unzipping his pants he pushed her thong to the side and pumped into her. She squeezed her eyes shut wishing he had locked the door. The desk was hard and uncomfortable. She also did her best to not move any of the items that were on it. She had started taking the pill ages ago, because Wyatt hated condoms. When he finished he handed her a couple of tissues from a shelf in the room, to clean up. He turned his back to her and straightened his suit as she did. Then asking her to sit he sat next to her and took her hands in his.

"Wow, I'm actually nervous" he began. Jane beamed thinking this is it. "I just want you to know that it has been really great dating for this past year" he went on. "I just want you to know that I think you are a great girl." He went on. She was thrilled hoping that after he had proposed they would announce to all the party goers. She imagined herself showing the ring to all the guests, Wyatt smiling broadly behind her. She would of course leave out the pre proposal sex, wishing it might have been more romantic. Her hands in his, she sat waiting to hear those four wonderful words.

Chapter Fourteen

I nstead, he promptly broke up with her. She blinked and felt her mouth fall open and she stared at him unsure if she had heard him correctly. He went on to explain that she was his college girlfriend and that he didn't want to be tied down right now. He knew that they had discussed her moving out to Chicago to be with him but he really didn't think that was fair to either of them. He thanked her for being a good girlfriend and wished her success in future relationships.

He modestly explained that he understood getting over him would probably take some time but he believed that she would be okay. He then said that it was all he had wanted to say to her and he hoped she enjoyed the rest of the evening. He stood holding out his hand to help her up and then lead her to the door. Once there, he shook her hand and said he needed to get back to his guests. She leaned against the door frame to aid her knees which she was not sure could hold her up at that moment.

She felt like she was on an airplane descending prior to landing. Her ears felt full of pressure and as though they needed to pop. The lights seemed brighter, like her eyes were adjusting as she was walking from a dark room into the afternoon sun. Her tongue felt suddenly bigger than her mouth, she wanted to open her lips and pant. She sucked in air like gulps of water, on a hot day, her chest rising and falling again and again.

Lacey saw her from across the room and rushed over. "I have to get out of here" was all Jane could muster. Linking arms they made their way to the door. Jane turned to wildly look for Wyatt before leaving. She found him and their eyes met, when he abruptly dropped her gaze and turned around. Lacey seeing this forcefully pulled Jane out the door. Jane would not say a word while they waited for the valet to bring Jane's car around.

Sensing Jane was clearly in no shape to drive Lacey took the keys from her, motioning her towards the passenger seat. "What happened?" she asked once they were on the way. "He broke up with me" Jane sobbed. This even surprised Lacey, who while no fan of Wyatt, could not even picture him doing this. She did her best to try to attempt to control her temper. There was some strong language being muttered but that was the best she could do. She drove to their, now almost empty, apartment.

Getting Jane inside she pulled out a couple of folding chairs from a closet that had been there since they moved in. Jane sat and kicked off her heels.

Lacey pushed her chair next to her and putting her arm around her said "I have absolutely no idea what to say to you right now. Do you want me to get you anything?"

"I am such a dumbass. I honestly thought he was going to propose to me tonight."

At that Lacey sucked in her breath. Wyatt went right back to the top of her shit list. Jane really didn't react much more that night. She seemed numb to what had happened. When she finally did say something it was just "I thought he was going to propose" over and over. Around 11pm, Lacey was seriously regretting bringing them to this mainly empty apartment.

Getting Jane back up she said "Look the only way we are getting any sleep here tonight is on the floor and I'm not into that. My new place is close by. Come on you are spending the night with me."

Jane went willingly and even confessed to being starved. So, on the way, Lacey popped through a drive through. Nothing like burgers and fries to heal a broken heart, she thought. At her apartment Jane dove into her food. Once done, she just looked exhausted. Lacey lent her some sweats and she passed out on her sofa.

Lacey purposely turned Jane's phone off and took it with her when she went to sleep. She didn't want Jane to have the opportunity to send any late night desperate pleas for reconciliation. Jane knew Lacey thought she was asleep but she wasn't. She just lay there unable to turn her mind off. Part of her just did not believe Wyatt. She knew him well enough to know that he was very fond of his routines. He would probably feel a sense of loss if they did not speak for a week and then end this silly break up.

That seemed like the only logical outcome Jane could come up with. Otherwise, no, she would not even consider the alternative. Happy that this was clearly only temporary, she sank into a deep peaceful sleep. She woke up refreshed the next morning and was enjoying a bowl of cereal and watching some TV when Lacey walked out of her room rubbing her eyes.

"Hey how are you doing?" she asked sitting down next to Jane.

"I'm great, it is supposed to be beautiful outside today.

We should go for a walk, maybe look for a sidewalk sale or something" she replied happily.

Lacey furrowed her brows and gave her a sidelined glance. This was not the type of reaction she was expecting.

"You sure you're okay?" she asked gently.

"Yep" Jane replied "I have to swing by my parent's house to shower and change first."

Lacey hopped into the shower and wore a sparkly tank top with some cut offs and hot pink flip flops. Grabbing her sunglasses she and Jane headed out the door. Jane hit a drive through on the way. Lacey got an egg sandwich and Jane helped herself to the hash browns and they both got iced coffees. It was a bit awkward once they got to Jane's parents house. Jane's mother rushed her, as soon as they entered the door, and asked her if Wyatt proposed. Jane informed her that he did not, but the party was lovely otherwise. Lacey held in the "HUH?" that she came very close to saying at that and did her best to just nod and smile.

When they got up to Jane's room she said "Why did you tell your mom the night was lovely? When it wasn't."

"I didn't want her to worry. Besides this is obviously just temporary" she replied.

Lacey's mouth dropped open. Jane smiled and grabbed a sundress and headed towards the bathroom. Lacey sat on her bed thinking this must clearly be denial and wondering, is a bad breakup not unlike trying to end a dependence on a drug? She mused maybe there should be a 12 step program for breakups. Jane was finished getting ready in no time.

"It's a bummer we didn't know you would be in town this summer, we could have stayed in our apartment" Lacey said as they were getting back into the car.

"Oh don't be silly I won't be here long" Jane answered.

Lacey, concerned remained quiet after that. They parked down town and checked out cute little shops and cafes. For lunch, they went to a local deep dish pizza place. Afterward they walked along the river then sat for a bit and people watched.

"Lace, do you think Wyatt and I will get back together?" Jane asked after a while.

"I really don't know babe" Lacey replied shrugging.

"I think we will" Jane said solemnly.

At that Lacey reached out and took her hand. "But what if you don't?" Lacey asked.

Jane just shook her head and looked forward.

"Wanna come over for dinner?" Jane asked.

"Free home cooked food" was all Lacey said in reply grinning.

Jane called her mom to give her a heads up and the two headed back to her house. They stopped along the way for Lacey to pick up her car. That way Jane would not have to drive her home after dinner.

Her mother had made a chicken rice and mushroom casserole with steamed green beans. Jane set the table while her mom finished up in the kitchen and Lacey sat in the den with Mr. Martin. Lacey loved Jane's dad, he was very cool. She sometimes scratched her head, how he could stay so laid back and still be married to Jane's mom. Either way, he gave really good advice and Lacey had picked his brain often over the years.

She contemplated telling him about what happened with Jane and Wyatt but, in the off chance that Jane was right, she held off. Mrs. Martin's cooking was delicious as usual. The conversation on the other hand was very stilted and uncomfortable. Mrs. Martin kept asking about Wyatt and when Jane was going to meet him in Chicago. Jane deflected each question noncommittally.

Her mother gave up and turned to ask Lacey about her plans for the summer. Lacey told them about the show she was in and offered to get them tickets, if they wanted to see it. It was officially starting that Thursday and had a 2 month run. It had an evening show Wednesday through Saturday with a matinee Saturday afternoon as well. She was really looking forward to it.

She went on to tell them about her new apartment as well. Lacey lit up with excitement, just talking about it. Jane was so proud of her friend. She was just bummed she wasn't as confident about her own future. After dinner Lacey hung out for a bit before heading home. After she left, Jane went to her room to unpack at bit more and think about things.

Chapter Fifteen

She could not actually consider an existence without Wyatt. He was all she knew and she could not bear the idea that the fantasy of their future life together would not come to be. The house they would live, the children they would have. She lay on her bed and looked around her room. Her eyes resting on her childhood state spoon collection. She rose and went over to where the display case was hung. Her fingers delicately brushing the porcelain handles.

It struck her all of sudden when she realized she did not have a spoon for Illinois. What if she were to take a road trip? She could possibly sell the idea of a right of passage summer trip after graduation to her parents. Jane and Lacey had once even talked about going to Australia, this was clearly an easy sell in comparison, There were a spattering of states across the country, she was missing spoons for. Her dad may even get a kick out of the thought she would finish the collection, he started for her.

That was a great idea she thought. Besides, what cross country road trip would be complete without a stop in

Chicago? Plus, if she was in Chicago she would see Wyatt. She stopped imagining her future without Wyatt and began imagining his face when she would tell him about her road trip. He would never believe it; it was too independent of a thing for her to do.

If he thought she was forging on, travelling and planning a life without him, of course it would make him want her back. She called Lacey to tell her the idea. Lacey loved it; she asked Jane if she would consider waiting until the end of her show because if she would Lacey would love to go too. Jane had not thought of that originally, but once Lacey brought it up, it made a lot of sense. It could be dangerous out there all by herself.

She just didn't know if she could wait two whole months living with her parents. Besides how would she play off not speaking to or visiting Wyatt for that long? Come on, this was Lacey she thought, of course she wanted to road trip with her.

"Sure" she said "that will give me plenty of time to plot out our route." Lacey made her promise not to over plan it. She agreed.

The thought of where they would go first and what they would see took her mind off of Wyatt for a while. She planned on running to a book store the next day to pick up some travel books. Now that she thought about it, there were places that she would love to see. She had heard there was a place in the Southwest where 4 states met at one point and she always wanted to see the Golden Gate Bridge.

The next morning, she woke up early and headed to the book store. She browsed the racks for a long time before settling on an AAA map book and 3 travel guides. Growing up in the South, she felt good about checking out other regions. She got a book on New England, the Mid

West and the Southwest. She got an iced coffee and sat outside flipping through her books.

They could start their trip heading west and see the Alamo, the 4 corners, then the Grand Canyon. After that they would head straight to the Pacific Ocean, drive along Ocean Drive and head right up to San Francisco and ride on a trolley. From there they could go to Las Vegas, she knew Lacey would love that. After Vegas they would go to Chicago and she would get to see Wyatt.

She did not plan on telling that part to Lacey. She was going to play it off, as wanting the see the museums she had studied while it was still in the plan for her to move there. Lacey knew how crazy she was about museums, she thought it was plausible. She still could not figure out how she was going to deal with waiting two whole months. She had thought planning the trip would take more time.

Plus she really did not want too much free time with her mother. It meant she would be asking her questions the whole time, questions Jane wanted to avoid. Also, road trips were not cheap. They would be hotels to pay for and food and gas. It was decided she needed a job.

She called Lacey and asked her where she should work. Lacey said she should totally be a nanny. That way she could work on her tan at the pool and watch daytime TV all day and she might even swing more money giving piano and or art lessons to the kids. Interesting Jane thought, but she was not sure she would be that great with kids. Then Lacey suggested temping.

Jane loved the idea because as a temp she could always turn down a position if something else was going on. After they hung up she called a temp agency and scheduled a meeting with them for the next day. Afterward she went to go broach the subject of a road trip with her parents. She spun it as sightseeing on her way to meet up with Wyatt and that she wasn't one hundred percent sure about moving in with him right away.

This way she could check out his place and the area in general before making her final decision. She felt bad for stretching the truth but it was the best she could do. She also told her parents she would be going with Lacey and depending on how the meeting tomorrow went would be tempting to raise money for the trip. Her father looked relieved at this news maybe thinking that she was expecting him to fund everything.

The next morning, she showered and dressed in a simple black suit with a teal shell and black flats. She wore her hair in a low ponytail at the nape of her neck. She joined her parents for breakfast and then headed to her appointment with the staffing agency.

When she got there, she completed a standard employment application. Then she took 3 computerized assessment tests. One test gauged her typing speed, another basic math skills and the last a memory evaluation. She was apparently successful in all and her employment coordinator had two opportunities available for her, that week.

The first was with a company that had a large mass mailing it was putting together, so she would be stuffing envelopes and sealing them all day for one week time frame. Another was with the same company just a different department and it would be the organization of their prior year files into boxes for storage. Both sounded reasonable, so she asked for the coordinator's opinion. Pleased to be trusted in such a fashion, the coordinator recommended the envelopes, as the filing job had a lot of heavy lifting.

"Sign me up" Jane replied.

She would start on Wednesday and would be off Saturday and Sunday returning the next week and finishing on Tuesday. Her coordinator gave her another tidbit. Apparently this company also had departments that utilized some temps long term. If she made a good impression at this posting it may offer her the ability to move into one of those roles.

That was great news, Jane thought. What she really wanted more than anything right now was to stay busy and out of her house. Wednesday was still 2 days away though, she would have to do something in the mean time. After her appointment, she stopped by the theatre where Lacey's show was playing.

They were rehearsing, but Jane was a familiar face so she was able to slip backstage and up to the upper catwalk. She waved at the audio/lighting guys in the control and sat down, watching from an opening where an unused spotlight was mounted. Lacey was upstage running a scene. Jane watched entranced.

"Hey stranger" a voice murmured in her ear.

She jumped knocking her head into the casing of the spotlight. "Ouch" she said rubbing her temple.

It was Jake, who she had helped paint previous sets with. "You scared the crap out of me" she said swatting his arm. He apologized saying that he had not meant to startle her. After that there was a bit of an awkward silence. Jane was never much of a conversationalist, outside of Lacey, Wyatt and her parents.

After a bit Jake asked "So what are your plans, now that you have graduated?"

She shrugged then said "They are kind of up in the air."

She went on to say she was starting a temp job and hopefully she and Lacey would be road tripping once the run was complete. Jake seemed to think that was pretty cool and asked where she thought they would go. Since Jane was in the very early planning stages she didn't know what to tell him and instead asked what he was doing over the summer. If she had remembered correctly, he was one year behind them in school. He was also in the theater arts program, as Lacey was, but studying the off stage craft versus what Lacey had studied.

It turned out this was a full time gig for him over the summer and the theatre. He was in charge of the lighting and had been checking other spotlights, when he ran into Jane. Otherwise he was just taking it easy over the summer probably going with friends to a lake house once the show was over. He confessed to also needing a hand if she wasn't busy that day.

Not doing anything else, she thought why not? She followed him down to a storage closet and helped him sort through lenses for the different lights. Some were in bad shape, so he needed to evaluate if it would be better just to replace them or if they were still serviceable. There were many different effects and colors used to give the feel of maybe different weather or times of day on stage.

She was enjoying herself so much she lost track of time and when he mentioned being starved, she checked her watch. It was past when her folks normally ate dinner, and since she had turned her cell phone to silent for her interview she had not heard her mom call. This whole being home by a certain time, like she was in high school again, it was going to take some getting used to. She apologized to Jake for having to run and went to look for Lacey.

Lacey was getting changed in the dressing room. Jane waved to her and asked if she wanted to grab a bite. As Lacey finished changing, Jane called her mother and explained why she had not heard the phone. Promising not to do it again, she gave her the good news about her meeting at the temp agency. With her mother now calm,

Jane let her know that she would be having dinner with Lace and would come home right after.

Leaving their cars where they were parked, the girls walked to a nearby Mexican place. Jane pulled the travel books out of her satchel, as they munched on chips and salsa while waiting for their food. Each with a book in hand, they called out interesting destinations they wanted to see on their road trip. When Jane brought up Chicago, Lacey became suspicious. She had known Jane far too long not to be.

Jane innocently shrugged at her and said that there were just many places there that seemed really interesting. Besides, hadn't Lacey herself always wondered if it really was that windy? Lacey dropped the subject but still wondered about it. They put the books away once their food arrived. Jane filled Lacey in on her employment success over dinner and told her how before she helped Jake, she was watching her rehearse.

"Lace, you looked amazing down there" Jane gushed.

Lacey, never one to shy away from praise, grinned "It felt really good today" she said.

After dinner Jane headed home. Her mother had already gone to bed with a book, and her father was watching TV in the living room.

"Hey Janey" he said as she sat across from him "Your mother told me about the job. I'm proud of you, kiddo."

"Dad" Jane moaned suddenly feeling 10 again.

He smiled and went back to watching his program. She watched for a bit with him but felt really tired and just went to bed and crashed. The next day, she focused on organizing her college things into her room, and laundry. She had all of her winter season stuff labeled and boxed, to be put in the attic. Then she started to purge some of her childhood relics that were taking up valuable surface space in her room.

Her hands lingered on a framed picture of her family on their trip to Paris. That was one of the happiest moments of her life. She allowed herself to rest in that memory for a beat. What she wanted more than anything else was to feel that type of excitement and joy again. For a fleeting moment, she acknowledged that she had never felt that way with Wyatt. She quickly banished that thought from her mind, thinking to herself that it was up to her to make that relationship work.

Even though she boxed up many mementos from her school years for storage she could not bring herself to pack that picture. She broke for lunch and had a sandwich with her mother, on their screen porch.

It was very pleasant until her mother asked "When was the last time you spoke to Wyatt?"

Jane mumbled something unintelligible in response.

"Jane is everything alright with the two of you?"

Unable to meet her mother's eyes, she shrugged.

"I knew it, I just knew something was wrong" her mother said standing up. "What did you do?" she demanded.

At that Jane crumpled and said that he just thought their relationship had run its course. Jane's mother thought that was a clear sign that he expected her to fight for him. To Jane that didn't sound like Wyatt at all. She tried to explain to her mother that he would consider fighting for him a sign of desperation.

Luckily her mother could see the logic in that.

"Well what are you going to do?" she asked.

Jane admitted she wasn't quite sure and had mainly planed to try to stay busy, so that if he did call or visit, she would not appear to be pining over him.

"What if he does not call or visit?" Mrs. Martin demanded.

Jane explained that she may be able to run into him, by chance, on her road trip with Lacey.

"Oh but if he sees you in Chicago after not hearing from you for a couple of months he will see he was wrong and try to get you back. "Very smart Jane."

Her mother sounded more proud of this plan, to get Wyatt back then she had been of Jane graduating college, Jane observed. At the very least her mother was now in complete support of the road trip. She even gave Jane a thumbs up, as she stood up to gather their plates. Jane rose to help her and cleared the rest of the table.

Chapter Sixteen

J ane spent the rest of the day doing laundry and organizing her room. After dinner with her folks, she called it an early night and went to bed. She wanted to be well rested for her first day of work. The next morning she didn't eat very much because she was so nervous. She packed a breakfast bar in her purse, in case she was starving later on.

When she got to the office building she was processed through Human Resources. They set her up with a temporary badge for the week and gave her a quick tour. She was then lead to the room where they were working on the mass mailing. The company that she was temping for was required to mail out any changes to their corporate terms to their clients, on an annual basis. They used temps for this function, because it was only done once per year.

The updated terms were in booklet form printed on tissue paper like sheets. The temps were tasked with trifolding an opt-out form and placing it with the booklet and a return envelope in another envelope. They were given trays to set the stuffed envelopes in. Once the trays were full, another temp would take them, and with a glue stick seal them all. After they were sealed, someone else would run the envelopes through a postage meter.

A couple of hours into her shift, Jane excused herself to go to the rest room. Once inside, she inhaled her breakfast bar. She was sure she had breaks, but so far the only temps to take one were the smokers. Once back in the room, she made small talk with a middle aged woman next to her. When it was time for lunch they walked across the street together for some fast food.

The rest of the day passed without anything interesting happening. Jane wasn't sure why she was so tired. It's true, it was manual labor, but on the extreme light side. When she got home she begged off dinner, ate a bowl of cereal, and went to bed. She was punctual, polite and a fast learner. By Thursday, it was clear she would be invited back to temp in a different department.

She was thrilled when she finished up on Friday looking forward to staying in her pjs, as long as possible, on Saturday. That night, Lacey's show opened, and she had reserved seats for Jane and her parents. The show was wonderful and afterward Jane went backstage to give Lacey a bouquet of flowers.

Jane's parents took them out for ice cream. It was a beautiful night and the girls sat on a wooden bench, and people watched while they enjoyed their waffle cones. Jane opted for White Chocolate Raspberry, while Lacey got Mint Chocolate Chip. Lacey was almost lit from within, high off of the adrenaline of her performance. Everything was beautiful or wonderful or amazing. Jane could not stop giggling at her.

When they were finished, Lacey walked them to the parking lot where both of their cars were parked. She let Jane and her parents know that her folks were going to be in town the following weekend, to see her show and wanted to know if they would like to all go out for dinner Wednesday night since Lacey did not have a performance that night.

Jane's parents accepted since they always got a kick out of Lacey's crazy mom. They even offered to put them up but Lacey was living downtown, they had picked a hotel close to her apartment. They said their goodbyes and returned home. Jane had no plans for Sunday. She went to the neighborhood pool and took a travel book.

On Monday she returned to the company where she had temped to be reprocessed for work in another department. This job was more open ended than the previous appointment. Now, she was doing data entry. This company maintained the software and customer service of retail stores check processing functions.

Jane was given photocopies of checks, and would enter the writers name, address, driver's license number and the check amount. They maintained this information and reconciled it against any checks that were returned by a writer's financial institution. By having this information, they were able to code the system to recognize the driver's license number of a writer who had bounced a check with any retail partner in their system.

If someone bounced a check one place, the system would decline their use of a check somewhere else. Jane was a decent typewriter, so she fit in well with this group. They were a mixture of full time employees and temps. Jane enjoyed this job, it was quiet and she was able to let her mind wander while she went in auto pilot with the data. With luck, she may be able to stay in this role until her road trip with Lacey.

Lacey was doing an amazing job as well in her show. A couple of local publications even did reviews and gave her raves. Things were good, but Jane could not help but be impatient. It had been weeks since her break with Wyatt. She had held out hope that he would have reached out to her, on his own by now. The fact that there had been no contact what so ever made her even more nervous about her plan. She did her best to shake off the nerves. It was the one thing that she had to be certain of to make it through this, and that was that she and Wyatt belonged together.

The weeks passed by. Lacey and Jane began their trip planning in earnest. They plotted out hotels and motels and in some situations bed and breakfasts that had high safety ratings. It was also important to them, as single girls to not travel too far off the beaten path. They were going to take Jane's car. About two weeks before their trip, Jane's dad took the car in for an overall. Oil change and transmission flushes, four new tires and any other recommended maintenance later he was satisfied the car was road trip worthy.

Jane's temp job went on till the Friday before their trip was starting. She had been such a good employee that the company even offered to take her back, once her road trip was done. She declined, with any luck she would be moving at the end of her trip. She went to both the matinee and final performance of Lacey's show to cheer her on. Once it was all complete and Lacey bowed, with tears streaming down her face.

Jane took her out for ice cream after. Part of her wanted to hit the road right then and there, Jane confessed. Lacey was cautiously optimistic that Jane was over Wyatt. She still had a sneaking suspicion about the stop in Illinois having something to do with Wyatt. She just felt that Jane had never dealt with the breakup.

She had been there for their prior breakup, and was

certain that Jane was avoiding this issue. She was able to talk Jane into waiting until Monday like they had originally planned. They both spent Sunday finishing packing. That night, Lacey spent the night at Jane's. After a complete breakfast, thanks to Jane's mom, they hit the road.

Chapter Seventeen

They headed south first. Lacey had found this place near Clearwater Florida called "Weeki Wachi" where you could see mermaids swim. They weren't actually mermaids, rather young women dressed up as mermaids performing an underwater show. Lacey's favorite movie of all time was the Little Mermaid, so it was the first sightseeing spot of their trip. Traffic south was light given it was a Monday, as opposed to Saturday and beach traffic.

The girls hope was to make it to Weeki Wachi in one swoop, the navigation system registered it as 13 hours away. Jane's mother had packed them a lunch for the first leg of their journey. Otherwise, they planned to eat via value menus on the road while attempting to avoid chain restaurants during their stops. Lacey could not resist a McDonald's Sweet Tea on their way out of town.

"You're going to regret getting an extra large ice tea babe" Jane said sliding into the driver's side as Lacey slurped happily away at her ginormous sweet tea. "We are only stopping two more times till Florida" Jane went on.

"I have the bladder of a camel. You do not scare me Jane Martin" Lacey said bravely.

Two hours later Lacey was dancing in her seat again. They had already stopped once for her, Jane grumbled about another unscheduled detour but smiling pulled off at the next exit anyway. Lacey took over driving after that, only to have greater control of her next bathroom break. Jane eventually dozed off and Lacey shook her awake for their last pit stop of the day. She groaned as she stretched her legs out, putting her hands on the small of her back, dipping her shoulders. She hoped she would not be this car sore the whole trip.

They arrived at the motel both very stiff. It was hot and humid, luckily the motel pool did not close until 10pm, the girls immediately grabbed their suits and went for a dip after checking in. The pool did wonders for their sore muscles. After an hour, or so they were exhausted and returned to their room. Jane called her parents to let them know they had arrived safely.

Other than the occasional giant flying roach, their room was decent, sparsely decorated with very creaky bed springs and thin mattresses. The next morning they took their time getting up and ready, as the mermaid show's first performance was not until 11am.

The show lasted an hour. It was something right out of an Esther Williams movie. Lacey loved every minute of it. On their way out of the park, they stopped by The Fudge Shop to eat a very unhealthy lunch before getting back on the road.

Lacey could not stop talking about the mermaid show. She wished she had recorded it, so she could watch it again and again. Although Jane didn't expect to enjoy it as much she felt the same way. Surprisingly, the show had reminded her of what she had felt that first trip to the Louvre. It was a feeling of simple bliss. Every little girl pretends to be a mermaid, while swimming in their local pools.

The girls stopped for coffee at a gas station on the way to Alabama Jane also picked up her first spoon of the trip. She did not need one for every state they were going to, but Florida happened to be one her collection was missing. She remembered as a kid wondering why they had never gone to Disney World, as it seemed every other child, she grew up with had. Their trip to New Orleans was leisurely and enjoyable, passing through Biloxi, laughing and singing along to the radio on the way.

When they finally arrived, and checked into their hotel they wandered to the Saint Louis cemetery. Jane was both struck by the artistic beauty of the above ground crypts, as she was completely creeped out by the whole thing. Lacey relived in the macabre of it all, it was then Jane predicted if Lacey ever got married it would be on Halloween. After they walked around for about an hour they made their way into the French Quarter. Jane refused to be anywhere near the cemetery at dusk. There was a famous cemetery near their school in Richmond called Hollywood Cemetery; neither of the girls had been and Jane promised to go there with Lacey someday, once back in Virginia.

They had delicious Cajun food and yummy drinks at French 75 Arnauds. Even though they were months late for Mardi Gras, Lacey still managed to get some beads for flashing her bra to some guys on Bourbon Street. From New Orleans they headed west to San Antonio Texas. The girls struggled to find anything but country music on the radio station. Over it Lacey turned the radio off and practiced her accents from around the world. Her Australian accent made Jane laugh so hard she cried as Lacey asked her over for a vegemite sandwich. Lacey pulled out some nail polish and started painting her toenails.

"Ugh, that stinks" Jane said cracking her window. "Can't you wait to do that at the motel?"

Lacey innocently replied "What if the check in clerk is an Ian Somerhalder look-a-like and does not fall madly in love with me because my toe nail polish is chipping?"

"It still stinks" Jane said laughing. "Who's Ian some-thing-something?"

"Other than my future spouse he is a super crush worthy vampire on this show I love" Jane gushed.

"Twilight?"

"No, those are movies, he's on a TV show" Lacey answered.

"Don't you have to pay for that channel?" Jane asked.

"Different vampire show, this one is on normal TV."

"I'm confused, I didn't realize vampires were so popular."

"Come on hot well dressed guys, who want to bite you, never age, never play beer pong and don't need to sleep. I think they will always be popular."

"Alright, alright. Just finish your toenails already, and maybe hang your feet out the window to dry." Jane said laughing.

They speed raced through the Alamo and ducked into some of the overly priced Ripley's Believe It Or Not museums to cool off. Eventually the girls made their way to the river walk, strolling along with ice cream and nipping in and out of shops. Jane managed to find a spoon she liked to add to her collection. Jane called her parents to say hello, her father thought it was great fun she had two more of her missing state spoons.

He jokingly made her promise not to try and to drive to Hawaii in search of that spoon. Laughing, she replied that she would not make that same promise for Alaska, though that might be for different road trip. Lacey had tried to talk Jane into going to Mexico, but Jane had seen all of the reports of Border Violence when she researched it online, and flat out refused. So, they headed towards Roswell New Mexico instead. Jane promised, someday when Lacey was a rich and famous actress, that she could take her on a private jet to Cabo. That put an end to that.

The purpose of heading to Roswell was for a laugh, that and it was a decent stopping point on their way to Santa Fe. They would take some pictures; look for aliens, stuff like that. They stayed at The Belmont and had dinner at a restaurant called Not of This World. They sadly did not locate Area 51 or any aliens. Jane was so excited to check out the very vibrant Art scene in Santa Fe the next day. It was only 4 hours from Roswell so they were there by lunchtime.

Enjoying local restaurants they found along their route they discovered that authentic southwestern food tasted so much better in the southwest than the places they had back in Virginia. They started the day at the Georgia O'Keefe Museum. Jane could have stayed there all day. A sleeping bag on the floor in front of Cottonwood Tree in Spring, and she would be perfectly happy. Lacey on the other hand made fast friends with some cute local guys and wanted to get back to the Inn they were staying at to dress up for that evening. They met up with the local boys at The Camel Rock Casino, which was just north of town. Having never gambled before, both girls were a bit nervous but smartly set a limit of $40 each to spend.

Nervous Jane started out on the 10 cent slots. After thirty minutes of that, Lacey talked her into playing 21. They held their own for about an hour or so, until Lacey was broke and Jane only had $5 left. On the way out of the casino she put it in a one dollar slot and won $100 dollars.

The way the girls celebrated, you would have thought it was ten thousand dollar jackpot.

Now flush Jane offered to treat for dinner. The group went to The Juan Siddi Theatre to see the flamenco dancers. Jane and Lacey had so much fun even though they had stayed out later than they had originally planned. They even considered staying in Santa Fe for an extra day but, when they both awoke the next morning they decided new adventures awaited them elsewhere so they went ahead and hit the road.

They drove about 5 hours to the Navajo Indian Reservation, hiked out to the Four Corners and took turns having their pictures taken with a limb in 4 different states. In Flagstaff Arizona., they stayed at a Bed and Breakfast this time. It was called the Starlight Pines B & B. The owners were beyond gracious. The room was gorgeous and beds so fluffy soft, by far the nicest place they had stayed on their journey so far.

They took in an evening show at the Historic Orpheum Theater. The next day they made the 6 hour journey to the great city of Los Angeles California. This was a real treat for them, as they had preplanned to splurge and had booked a room at the Millennium Biltmore Hotel. It cost more than any other place they stayed on the entirety of their trip but was a steal in comparison to some of the other historic hotels, in LA. The Biltmore was built in 1923 and was located where the Oscar Awards concept was created. Where else could a budding actress stay? Just walking through its beautiful arched doorway Lacey felt like she was walking into another time. The lobby alone was so incredible that, instead of checking in right away, they sat down in big cushy wing chairs and just took it all in.

Both girls enjoyed LA. It was different then it seems in

movies, but all the sites were there. The Hollywood sign, The Walk of Fame, Rodeo Drive and all of the stores well over their budget. The girls for the first time were introduced to In and Out Burgers, which turned out to be an amazing burger. That evening they headed north towards Santa Cruz. What better way to watch a sunset then from The Pacific Coast Highway, the road that runs along the coast for most the length of California. The girls weren't in a hurry, as the next day was a beach day.

The Pacific Ocean had much bigger waves compared to the Atlantic. They sat and watched surfers perform maneuvers that could have come out of any Hollywood movie they had ever seen, or been a cover of a surfer magazine. There were, of course, also the less successful surfers. What amazed Jane, were the younger surfers. Some of these kids could not have been older than 8. They showed no fear, as they took the waves with abandon.

Jane watched awestruck and had a question for herself, if she had ever felt like that. The answer was no. The whole point of this trip had been an excuse to get back together with Wyatt for her. She had to acknowledge to herself if nothing else that the closer they got to Chicago the less she felt like going there. She pushed that thought away. Wyatt was her future. If they did not get back together, what would she do?

They were too tired from all the sun to head straight to San Francisco that night so they stayed another night in Santa Cruz and hit the road early. San Francisco was not far and it did not alter their schedule too much by staying. Once in San Francisco, they drove down the famous Lombard Street.

They then found a centrally located parking place and walked to Fisherman's Wharf. While touring Alcatraz, they took turns taking pictures of each other in jail cells making silly faces. They both wore headsets and the speaker had the most monotone voice. By the end of the tour they had both stopped listening and Lacey was inventing wild facts about the prison that had Jane clutching her sides she was laughing so hard. Their antics drew stern looks from staff and stifling their giggles they were on their best behavior till they returned to the mainland.

For a late lunch, they each had a bowl of clam chowder in a bread bowl. Someone along the way had said it was a wharf staple. Some of the best advice they had ever taken. After lunch they had planned to walk across the Golden Gate Bridge. As they made their way over there they realized just how big of a walk they were getting themselves into and agreed to instead walk onto the bridge then back off of it. All the walking at the Wharf and Alcatraz had taken it out of them.

Chapter Eighteen

After leaving San Francisco, the girls headed towards Las Vegas Nevada. Although still physically exhausted from all the walking the day before, they got up early to beat the rush hour traffic out of San Francisco. They pulled onto the Strip in Vegas around 4pm later that day. They were stayed at the old end of the strip, for a ridiculous $25 bucks. They didn't gamble much, mostly came to see the lights and people watch. They strolled the strip and had dinner at the Paris Café before going to see one of the Cirque du Soleil shows. Jane's mom had bought them the tickets for the show, it was like nothing they had ever seen.

Over the years PBS would televise different performances live from Las Vegas during different fund raising campaigns. Seeing it live though, was something else all together. Lacey sat mouth open and Jane kept holding her breath, not wanting to make any movement or noise and take anything away from the performance. They were the only ones left in the theatre they had not moved from their seats for a full ten minutes after final bows saying "Oh my God" over and over again.

They ended their evening with the light show on Fremont Street. On their walk back to their hotel Lacey vowed to someday live in Vegas. The city had found a new diehard fan. Jane thought it was a fun city, but she knew she would never want to live there. It was like sensory overload and almost made her head hurt. She almost wished she was back in Santa Cruz feeling the sun on her back, watching surfers.

They stopped in Park City, Utah next, it was the home of the Sundance Film Festival. The festival was in January, not August, but still there were plenty of things to do there. Besides where the festival was held, even if in the wrong month was enough for Lacey. They went and saw a movie too, just so she could honestly say she went to a screening at Sundance.

It was beautiful country as well; it was easy to see why celebrities wanted to live there. They stayed in another bed and breakfast. It wasn't as amazing as the one in Flagstaff but that place had set the bar pretty high. They both phoned their parents. Jane got a bit of a lecture, since her folks had expected to hear from her more often. She promised to be better about it going forward, they just had been so busy. They went to take pictures of The Great Salt Lake that the city was named after, and then made their way west to Denver.

They were going to spend the day at The Clyfford Still Museum. He had been a professor, at their University. This was one of the things Jane adored about Art History. How one artist could have made an impact in so many different areas? She was also a huge fan of his work.

Lacey was a good sport, even though art museums were not really her thing. She was just content to see Jane so happy. Besides, after their night in Denver their next stop would be house. Her parents lived in a town called Irwin that was northwest of Des Moines Iowa. Her father was treating them to two days at the spa. After all of the driving, they had been doing, Lacey could not wait for a long soak and a massage.

Her mom was now into carving. She had her father trekking through the woods around their home looking for fallen trees. Lacey shook her head at them. At least her pieces were now taking up less yard space. Some of her smaller pieces were actually quite charming even though neither Lacey nor Jane could tell what they were.

The first day at the spa both Lacey and Jane fell asleep in their mud baths. Heading to the showers to rinse off, Lacey asked Jane why they were really going to Chicago. Jane, still drowsy from her nap, shrugged and looked away quickly. Caught Lacey thought. She spent the rest of the day trying to talk Jane out of it enough though she knew it was futile.

Jane could be so stubborn when it came to things that made absolutely no sense. Lacey wanted to shake her friend. Jane was having extreme tunnel vision, and unfortunately the only thing at the end of it was Wyatt. Even she was unable to put into words why she even wanted to be with him at all. Lacey gave up hoping, even though it would cause Jane pain in the short term that Wyatt really was done with her.

They didn't really speak to each other the second day in Iowa. Jane felt defensive and Lacey felt sorry for her. By the end of that day, Lacey caved and said whatever happened she would respect her decision, even if she did not agree with it. Jane readily forgave her, because she could never stay angry at Lacey for too long. Lacey's parents planned a big dinner in their honor. They invited a bunch of Lacey's friends from high school and their neighbors. Before the night was over, Lacey's mother gave them each a small carving she had made.

She explained that the carvings worked both separately and together. They were, individually, each a female figure. Jane's stood with one arm gently on her hip and the other over her heart. Lacey's had one arm stretched out to her side and the other crossing over in front of her. The outstretched arm of Lacey's figure fit perfectly through the nook made on the side of Jane's figure, where her hand was placed on her hip. The other arm crossing her body rested on Jane's figures hand covering its heart. They were beautiful both apart but even more so together. It brought Lacey to tears. She embraced her mother realizing that, while her mother did seem out of it more often than not, at the end of the day she got her.

Seeing Lacey cry made Jane cry and sniffling they hugged each other. Any awkwardness from earlier now completely gone. The next morning they took their time over breakfast and saying their goodbyes to Lacey's parents. Lacey and her mother gave each other an extra long hug.

There was a comfortable silence on their drive to Chicago. They were there by dinner time and checked into their hotel. They were staying at the Best Western Downtown, which of course broke their national chain rule, but most hotels were expensive in Chicago. This was the only way they were going to afford a place overlooking Lake Michigan.

On the way to the hotel, they had a heart to heart as to what Jane's true plan for Chicago was. She knew Wyatt would be living downtown, not far from his school. She would text him, when they got to their hotel to let him know she was in town and ask him if he wanted to meet up. Hopefully they would meet for lunch, he would admit his error in ending things and they would be back together by dessert. Meanwhile Lacey would go sightseeing at Navy Pier.

Everything went to plan and Jane met Wyatt the next day at Petterino's. She had chosen one of his favorite dresses to wear and Lacey had to admit she looked beautiful. He would be a fool to not see that for himself. Jane arrived at the restaurant before him and, since they had reservations, was seated first. The table had three settings, Jane tried to tell the hostess there was a mistake but stopped when she saw Wyatt arrive with a guest.

Chapter Nineteen

The air left her body and she tried her best to inhale as she watched Wyatt approach the table holding the hand of a gut wrenchingly beautiful girl. He was holding her hand. Jane could not believe what she was seeing. They had only been on a break. He was supposed to have seen Jane and want to be with her. Instead he was pulling the chair out for another girl.

Wyatt introduced Blythe Carlisle, his girlfriend, to Jane. It took every ounce of strength for Jane not to burst into tears on the spot. When she saw Wyatt observing her for this very response her will hardened. She suddenly behaved as she had at every mixer her mother had ever thrown. She was the epitome of grace. She regaled them with stories of her trip with Lacey, looking Wyatt directly in the eyes.

She wanted more than anything else to show him she was not broken. At one point, when Blythe rose to go to the ladies, Wyatt had the nerve to ask Jane if she wanted to fuck. Blythe had errands to run after lunch and he could do her in his car for old time's sake, if she wanted. She almost left right then but Blythe was already returning so she stayed put.

When their meal was done, Wyatt even invited her to go out with them that evening. She waved him off explaining she and Lacey already had plans, that she had only left lunch free to see him. She reveled in how taken aback that comment caught him. She smiled sweetly kissing Blythe on both cheeks and only waved at Wyatt, when he had clearly opened his arms for an embrace, before she left. She felt a final victory in that.

She walked away in tears, vowing not to look back. Jane sent Lacey a S.O.S text and headed straight back to their hotel. Lacey met her there about 30 minutes later. Jane was a mess. She sat on the floor, in her pretty dress, shaking with tears. Her mascara which claimed to be waterproof ran in faint lines down her cheeks.

"What happened?" Lacey exclaimed rushing to her.

When Jane spoke, she sucked in a breath after each word. "He...brought....his...new....girlfriend.....and when ....she was .....in the .....bathroom .....he asked.... me if I ...wanted to ...do it" she sobbed.

Lacey rubbed her back and let her cry it out. When Jane was calmer, she wiped the makeup off her face, and brushed and braided her hair. Lacey ran a bath for Jane, it clear her friend need a long hot soak. Lacey even sprang for room service and ordered Jane's favorite, a deep Belgian style waffle topped with powdered sugar, with strawberries and cantaloupe on the side. Jane had no appetite but seeing how much Lacey shelled out for the food, ate it all. Her mind was racing, she was so depressed and angry at the same time.

Wyatt had ambushed her. He should have told her, he was first bringing someone and second that someone was his new girlfriend. At the very least, she was proud of herself that she had been able to hold it together. For that part alone, she had no regret. Jane went to sleep before Lacey and sniffled every so often. Each time she did Lacey would look over at her to see if she was still asleep. The next morning when Lacey awoke, Jane was sitting on the edge of her bed just looking at her. It was kind of creepy but forgivable.

"Lace" she began "what am I going to do?"

Lacey sat up and asked "Today? Or like for life?"

Jane shrugged in response.

Lacey smiled "We're young babe, you don't have to know.""

I just don't understand why he doesn't love me anymore" Jane signed. She looked up her eyes brimming with tears "I still love him so much it hurts."

What she wanted to say was 'How, how can you love that asshole' but that would not have gone over well, so biting her lip she said

"Shh, shh. It will be okay sweetie."

They had been on the road for over 3 weeks and had planned to go to New York and then New England next. Lacey made an executive decision, that they were instead going to Dolly wood. They would stop in Nashville, on the way down, and then go on to Dolly wood. She was certain this would cheer Jane up better than anything else.

Not up for arguing, Jane agreed to the schedule change. Someday she would make it to the Brandywine River Museum but her heart just wasn't in it, right now. She truly just wanted to go straight home but didn't want to break the news to her mother either. Lacey drove the whole way this leg.

Jane sat silently in the passenger seat staring out the side window at the passing landscape. From time to time she would sniffle but otherwise she just seemed vacant.

Lacey would grab her knee and shake it while checking on her.

Jane would look over at her and give a very weak half smile and shrug then, as if looking at Lacey were too much she would deeply inhale and shudder out her breath. She refused food the two times they stopped for gas or bathroom breaks. She felt as though if she even tried to eat something she would be sick.

She could not get the image of Wyatt and that girl out of her mind. It made her feel inferior. That girl was so beautiful and she seemed so polished during lunch. Wyatt had even held her hand on top of the table while they waited for their order. He had never done that with Jane. What was wrong with her, she wondered? Why couldn't she be what he wanted?

Lacey was able to get them a room at the Hotel Preston which was easy to get to near the airport. They stopped by the Parthenon, on the way to Dolly Wood. Jane barely glanced at it so they did not linger. Once at Dolly Wood, Lacey dragged Jane onto every rollercoaster. By the end of the day and after a funnel cake, Jane was full of adrenaline and not as moopy.

Lacey had gotten them a room at The Roaring Fork. Jane lay down the moment they were in the room.

"Feel like talking?" Lacey asked gently.

Jane shook her head.

"I'm going to take a quick shower then maybe we can watch a movie." Lacey said heading for the bathroom.

Jane laid there listening to the sound of the running water. 'What had gone wrong' she thought to herself. She was in such foreign territory of being in limbo, or something even worse than limbo, a seemingly endless plain of unknown. Her insecurities took hold and began chewing away at the careful exterior she had built up around herself in her belief that this break up was temporary.

Her chest felt tight, and she sat up in an effort to take deeper breathes. Lacey, done with her shower walked back into the main room already dressed for bed towel drying her hair. The sound of Jane labored breathing had been drowned out by the fan in the bathroom.

"Babe" Lacey boomed as she crossed the room and began rubbing Jane on the back. "Here" she said pulling Jane's knees up "put your head between your knees. Alright, deep breathes."

Jane slowly stopped hyperventilating and asked for some water. Her throat felt raw and even though her head was still between her knees she felt dizzy. Lacey rushed back with a coffee mug of sink water. Lifting her head Jane took baby sips, the water burned going down and she handed the mug to Lacey then ran to the bathroom feeling nauseous. She emptied her stomach and gagged as body tried desperately to rid her of food that was not there.

Lacey her ever vigil nurse held a cool washcloth to her neck until she was done. Sure she was done Jane shakily got to her feet and rinsed her mouth with hotel mouthwash. Lacey had gone in search of Ginger Ale. Jane stood there at the sink and appraised herself in the mirror. It seemed so obvious at that moment. Of course Wyatt would not want her back, just look at her. A part of her had always wondered why Wyatt ever seemed to like her. Her mind began to twirl on repeat a cadence of everything she disliked about herself; she was ugly, her forehead was too big, she didn't have a six pack, she wasn't smart. What if he had never cared about her? or maybe their whole relationship has been a joke to him.

Jane suddenly felt repulsed by her own reflection, she turned away feeling sick again. Being with Wyatt had somehow validated her, she had measured herself by his opinion of her. She stumbled back into the main room just as Lacey burst through the door triumphantly brandishing a can of Seagrams ginger ale.

Lacey's glee faltered when she caught Jane's eye. "Still feel sick? I come bearing a magical tummy ache cure" she said popping the top

Jane sank to the floor and sobbed in earnest. Lacey came to sit with her and did her best to get Jane to talk. Unfortunately, Jane just could not find the words to explain the pain she was feeling. She supposed to be in Chicago right now, with Wyatt. They were going to be a team, he was supposed to want her. The thought that he not only did not want her but had already replaced her brought her to a level of inferiority she did not know existed.

As she sat on the floor with Lacey's arms around her she sagged further just without energy to cry anymore. She shrugged out of Lacey's embrace and crawled up onto her bed. Lacey came to sit by her and smoothed her hair away from her face. Jane fell asleep and Lacey folded the coverlet over her. She staggered to her own bed and peered at the alarm clock in the room before turning out the night. It felt later than it actually was. The emotions of that night clearly exhausted them both.

Jane awoke before Lacey and went to the bathroom. Her eyes and nose were red from all of her crying. She brushed her teeth and went to take a shower. She starting going through the motions, shampoo in hair, lather, soap on body, and rinse. She wondered why she was even bothering. Feeling all at once overwhelmed she sat down and let the water cascade all around her. There was a part of her that wanted to give up all together, find a place where it would not hurt anymore. Jane sat there and considered taking her own life.

If she were to do it, how would she? The concept of physical pain terrified her which ruled out most options. The idea of taking something and just falling sleep and never waking up again appealed to her. She was pulled from her morbid considerations by Lacey poking her head around the bathroom door.

"You okay?" she said, "you've been in there for a long time."

Jane jumped to her feet and turned off the water. "Lost track of time" she mumbled grabbing a towel.

"Want to stay here another night, or head home?" Lacey asked.

"I don't know" Jane admitted.

"Let's stay one more day, maybe get some food into you and maybe talk" Lacey suggested.

Jane nodded and went to get dressed while Lacey went to the bathroom. She put on a t-shirt and yoga pants. Not bothering to dry her hair she twisted it up in a bun. She reeled at what her train of thoughts in the shower had been. Was she losing it? she wondered to herself. She rubbed her arms suddenly chilled.

"Cold?" Lacey asked walking out of the bathroom "I can turn off the AC."

"Just got the chills. I'm fine" Jane replied.

"Well I'm starved. Do you think you can eat anything?" Lacey asked still in nurse mode.

"I could go for a bagel" Jane admitted "does this place have a breakfast bar?"

"No way, let's go someplace we can be sure the bagels are fresh. I think I saw a bakery in town." Lacey declared.

Not one to argue with fresh bagels Jane agreed. Lacey found the bakery, Jane ordered cinnamon raison while Lacey got an everything bagel. Jane delicately picked at hers while Lacey did her best to consume hers in a few bites as possible.

"What?" she mumbled with a full mouth "we skipped dinner last night."

Jane could not help but giggle. Maybe she would be okay Jane thought to herself. That was until a young couple strolled in. At the counter the guy casually wrapped his arm on the girl's shoulder as she leaned into him. They looked so together it struck Jane with the concept of how alone she was. Lacey saw her expression fall and followed her gaze to the couple.

Seeing the tears brimming in Jane's eyes she gathered up what was left of Jane's bagel and said "Hey let's head back to the hotel."

Jane nodded and followed Lacey to the car. She was able to hold herself together until she was safely in the car. Tears streaming down her face she searched for a napkin to wipe her nose. Lacey quietly drove back to the hotel. Her quiet unnerved Jane who just was not used to it.

"Lacey, what is wrong with me?" Jane sobbed.

"Nothing is wrong with you Jane" Lacey soothed "you just need to realize that."

Back in the room Lacey tried to convince Jane to finish her bagel. She continued to nibble at it just to make Lacey happy.

Lacey paced back and forth. Finally stopping she turned to Jane and said "I blame myself for all of this you know."

"What?" Jane replied confused.

"If I would have never introduced you to that asshole you would not be dealing with this. I will never understand what you saw in him but you just have to know how special and beautiful, and talented you are. I know you are hurting right now, I get that, I just wish you could see what a tool he was and know that you deserve so much better." Lacey said pleadingly.

Jane shook her head, Lacey just didn't understand. Wyatt was her life, they were going to get married, have children and grow old together. No one had ever shown the type of interest in her that he had and she was sure that no one else ever would. When she said as much to Lacey she jumped all over her and reminded her to stop living in the past. Yes, she was southern and her example was her mother, a woman who never worked. She had to recognize how unrealistic that was in this day and age. Sometimes Jane wished she lived in another era. Lacey looked at her as though she had grown an extra head and confessed she could never live without her smart phone.

The day went on like that, Jane would cry and Lacey would do her best to cheer her up. Lacey was just at a loss of what to do. Finally they decided that they would head back to Richmond in the morning. As much as Jane loved Lacey, she just wanted to be at home in her own bed, with her blanket pulled over her head. Lacey ran out at lunchtime and got them each sandwiches. Jane actually ate hers, finally hungry. Full from lunch they skipped dinner. They stayed up far too late, talking. The next morning Jane almost felt hung over trying to wake up. They had breakfast at a little diner and then hit the road yet again.

On the road they discussed Jane's plans for the future. Not able to admit becoming a recluse was her main plan Jane stayed quiet.

"Would you want to live with me?" Lacey asked arching a brow.

"Versus living with my parents? Um yeah, but I don't think I want to go to New York either."

Lacey had loosely been planning to move there in the fall.

"What if I put off New York for a bit?" Lacey offered.

"Absolutely not" Jane said shaking her head. "We will just have to Skype, besides maybe what I really need is to, for the first time in my life, live by myself."

The moment she said it out loud she knew since asking Lacey to postpone going after her dream wasn't an option this was the right choice. She felt like her whole life, she had to a certain extent done whatever someone else wanted her to do. Her mother, Wyatt, sometimes even Lacey. Even if she thought it was for her own good, case in point Dolly wood. Lacey felt the truth in what Jane had said as well. It was just hard to not want to help her. Jane was her best friend, she worried about her.

When they pulled up to Jane's house, Lacey would stay for dinner but then drive her car which she had left at the Martin's for their trip home. Jane's parents were shocked they were home so soon, as they had not expected them for another two weeks at least. Lacey discretely explained that Jane wasn't feeling well so they shortened the trip skipping their planed stops in New England. Jane's mother got to cooking and they had fried chicken, corn on the cob and potato salad on the Martin's screen porch.

Over dinner Jane broke the news to her mother about Wyatt. Her mother, while visibly surprised, took it well. Mr. Martin, who had not been aware of the plot to reunite with Wyatt gaped at Jane's mother. Mrs. Martin blushed under his gaze and mumbled something about it being what Jane wanted. He sat through the rest of dinner with a grim expression on his face. From time to time he would reach out and pat Jane's hand when she rested it on the table. His sympathy made her want to cry all over again. All Jane wanted to do was lay down. After Lacey left that is exactly what she did.

She avoided Lacey's calls and her parent's attempts to

discuss her future that first week back. She mooned over pictures and mementos from her time with Wyatt. Her diet consisted mainly of pop tarts and ice cream. By the end of the week she finally started to contemplate life outside of her parent's house. Maybe if she had her own place we would not have to deal with the constant questions how was she doing, or all of the advice she did not ask for. Her dad at one point even felt necessary to tell her they were other fish in the sea.

Jane hoped to find an inexpensive place near the university. True, that meant she may have loud neighbors, but it was fairly safe and less expensive there. Her father could not fault her logic but suggested given the current economy, she stay at home a couple of months to build up an emergency fund. That way she would have 4 months of rent saved up in the off chance she was not able to work a full month, since her work was not guaranteed.

He also asked if he could inquire among his colleagues, if any of them were hiring full time. It would be much more prudent for her to have full time employment, before she moved out. While this delay was not what she wanted, it was important to her to prove to her parents she was responsible enough to wait till the time was right.

Lacey would be moving in only 2 weeks. Jane would miss her more than anything but knew this move was a big step for her. Lacey would be crashing on the sofa of a former classmate, who had graduated a couple of years ahead of her. She could live with her for 3 months rent free. Lacey also saw this move as a test.

She did not expect to get hired in anything right away. She did want to take the time to go on as many auditions as possible. Similar to what you may hear a prospective bride trying on the perfect dress or someone buying a new car she mainly wanted to try New York on and see if it fit. If it did she had no doubt she could thrive. If it did not, she also had no issue packing it and trying something else.

It was also probably better for Jane that Lacey not be there, while Jane tested her own waters of independence. Lacey had a habit of mothering her. She just hated the thought of Jane in pain. She was the sister she had always wanted, there was a bond between them that they had nurtured and was stronger than ever.

Jane returned to her room and pulled out her laptop. She sent an email, to the manager of the place where she had temped, to see if there were any openings. With any luck, she may know something by the middle of the week. After that, she searched open positions near downtown. It was pretty slim pickings. She sent an email to a couple of her favorite professors to see if any of them were hiring an assistant.

She closed her laptop and shut her eyes trying to visualize what she wanted out of life. She even considered making one of those dream boards she had heard people talk about. You take or cut out pictures of the things you want to achieve in life and place them on a cork board as a constant reminder. It is supposed to help bring those dreams to fruition.

Jane's problem was she wouldn't even know what to cut out. She wanted an apartment but that would really only depend on what was available when she actually moved out. She also wanted a job but not to actually work just to afford the apartment. That would be the most depressing dream board ever. A cover of a For Rent magazine and a dollar sign.

She closed her eyes tight and whispered a wish out loud "I just want to be happy." The weight of her wish lifted off of her like a whoosh. She slept like a baby after that. She had thought being in her own bed after so long would have felt strange. She was wrong, it was amazing.

It was past 10 when she finally woke up and staggered to the kitchen. Her mother raised a brow at her and gestured to the coffee machine. Yum Jane thought, her parents always had the good flavored coffee creamers. She made herself a cup and went to sit with her mother.

"Would you like some toast with jam?" her mother asked.

"Yes, please" Jane said.

She sat with her mother as she enjoyed her toast and coffee.

"Plans for the day?" Mrs. Martin asked.

"Maybe go to the pool, wanna come?" Jane replied.

Her mother looked thrilled for the invite and accepted. Her father was out playing golf with some of his buddies so her mom was happy to get out of the house. They changed and grabbed their pool stuff and left. After getting bored with her book Jane turned to regard her mother. She was in her early fifties and had aged well. She seemed to still love Jane's dad. She would catch him patting her butt or winking at her from time to time so she assumed he was still happy with her. They had been married for almost 30 years. How do you find that, she wondered?

Her mother feeling Jane's gaze said "Everything ok Jane?"

Feeling tears threatening Jane nodded briskly, and got up to compose herself in the ladies room. She splashed cool water on her face and rubbed her neck, stretching it from side to side. Jane returned to the pool deck, and wanting to cool off dove into the pool.

She swam under water seeing how far she could go without taking a breath. She got about halfway before surfacing. She wiped her eyes, as she deeply inhaled and exhaled until she was breathing normal again. She waded over to the edge and returned to her lounge.

"Just cooling off" she said to her mother.

She lay back down and returned to her book. An hour later, her mother complaining of the heat, suggested they leave. Jane got up and gathered her things and quietly followed her mother home. Feeling drained, she laid down, after changing, in the living room. Her mother came to sit with her and brought her some iced tea. She dozed as her mother watched a show about gardening. Her father found them like that, when he returned from his golf outing.

"Great news Janey" he boomed from the doorway startling her. "Oh I didn't realize you were asleep, scoot over" he said patting her leg.

She sat up and rubbed her eyes "Hey dad, what's up?"

"I ran into Mark Hamilton at the golf course" he said happily.

He did this all the time. He would start a conversation in a way that made absolutely no sense to her. She did not know who Mark Hamilton or how her dad knew him so she shrugged in response.

He then looked expectedly at Mrs. Martin. "Remember Mark Hamilton, dear?"

She frowned and furrowed her brows trying to place him.

Exasperated he went on "We were in the same fraternity at school."

"Oh Mark Hamilton." her mother said smiling.

"Yes, and his assistant is retiring. He has not hired her replacement" he said beaming to Jane.

"Really?" Jane said putting one and one together.

"Yep, if you are interested. It does not start for another month or so, but I'm pretty sure it pays more than the temp place and you would get benefits and a 401k."

This was great news, Jane jumped up to give him a hug. She still had not heard back from the temp place by that Monday, so she tried to do something she had not done in a long time, draw. She first went to have her fake nails removed. Her own nails were thin and weak, but she had the nail tech coat them with some clear nail strengthening polish and made a mental note to pick some up as well.

At a traffic signal on the way back to her parents house with the palms of her hand on the wheel, she unfolded her fingers and just looked at her nails. She thought how they were not unlike herself. Thin and weak but she mused maybe not forever.

Chapter Twenty

At home she pulled out her sketch pad and pastels from a box in her room. She went to a local park, and sitting on a bench, looked around to see if there was anything interesting to draw. There was an older man fishing not far from her so she began with him. Her first attempt was laughable. Thankfully he mainly sat still so turning the page in her book she began again. Her second try was not much better. She tried to think why she was having such a problem with this. All at once it came to her. In the past when she drew she would almost turn her brain off, right now though she felt her thoughts drifting again and to Wyatt.

It made her feel ashamed. He clearly did not want her, why couldn't she stop thinking about him. It was almost like a compulsion. There were things that would trigger memories as well, like seeing a couple or seeing something in the news about his father. What she would never admit aloud to anyone including Lacey was a fear that no one else would love her.

Wyatt had been her first real boyfriend. She had imagined they would spend the rest of their lives together. The unchartered territory she currently found herself in was her own personal den of shame. Feeling tears threatening, she flipped her pad closed and hurried home. She retreated to her room and shut the door. Laying on her bed with her blankets pulled up to her nose, she quietly cried.

Her mother knocked on her door after hearing her cry from the hallway.

"Jane, why are you crying?" she said coming to sit by her and stroking her hair.

Jane just shook her head and buried her face into her pillow.

"Do you want to talk about it?" she continued.

Jane once again shook her head so her mother gave up and left her alone.

She felt as though no one could understand what she was feeling like maybe she hurt more because she loved more. She pictured Wyatt's new girlfriend and could not help but feel inferior in comparison. Blythe was so pretty and stylish, Jane ached inwardly thinking of how Wyatt probably thought the same thing. She also imagined his parents fawning over her and thanking their lucky stars that Wyatt had dumped her.

When her father got home from work after clearly talking to her mother, he came in to check on her.

"How we doing Janey?" he asked standing at the end of her bed.

She sat up and shrugged her shoulders at him.

"Is this to do with that Wyatt boy?" he asked.

She glumly nodded her head and then wiped her eyes.

"I say good riddance" he said gruffly surprising her. "Look I know you cared about that boy a great deal but I just need you to know that in my personal opinion he was not worth your time"

Jane's mouth dropped open.

Every girl wanted Wyatt, how could her father not see how wonderful he was? Maybe that was it was because he was her father so he was supposed to say stuff like that.

"You know maybe you would have a new boyfriend if you got out of bed" he went on.

Jane covered her face with a pillow and groaned.

Seeing that his pep talk was not having its intended result, he came over and kissed her on the top of her head and leaving the room said "Make sure you eat some dinner honey."

She got up and came to the table for dinner. Her mother had made spaghetti with meat sauce. Jane ate some and then just picked at it. Her mother offered her some garlic bread but she shook her head and drank some milk instead.

Her father perking up said "Hey your mother told me about this retail therapy thing. You want some cash to go shopping, maybe buy some new outfits for your new job?"

Her parents both looked at her with huge smiles like they really thought a trip to the mall would help her get over Wyatt. When she shook her head no her mother placed her hand to her chest and shot Mr. Martin a look of shock. Clearly this was more serious than Mrs. Martin had thought. After dinner Jane excused herself and went back to lay in her room. She still had not heard from the temp agency, so she was beginning to think she would be stuck here all day everyday for the next month. She cried herself to sleep. Sometime around 10am the next morning she awoke to Lacey opening her blinds.

"Rise and shine beautiful" she chirped pulling Jane's blanket from her. "I am only in town for 2 more weeks and I'll be damned if you spend them in your room" Lacey said, smacking her on the ass "Get your butt into the shower your dad gave me his credit card and said I could get some stuff too, so whether you like it or not we are going shopping."

"Leave me alone" Jane grumbled trying to cover herself with her sheet.

"No way, I can't shop unless you do too" Lacey returned.

Seeing that resistance was futile Jane got up and showered. She dressed in a t shirt, capris and flip flops. Lacey drove them to a popular outdoor style mall.

"Your parents are pretty worried about you, babe, and from what they told me, I'm with them. What set you off?" Lacey asked as they parked.

Not wanting to start crying again, Jane took a couple of deep breaths and said "I can't stop thinking about him. Yesterday I tried to go out and sketch something and I couldn't even focus on anything else."

"Time heals all wounds" Lacey said solemnly "and shopping helps." She winked at her and they got out

Walking into the mall, they passed by a hair salon. Jane stopped and looked at herself in the glass and toyed with her pony tail.

"Oh my God you should totally cut your hair." Lacey gushed.

Jane just shook her head and kept walking forward. They went into a popular clothing store with the goal of getting Jane some stuff for her new job. She camped out in a dressing room while Lacey and an employee of the store fed her a seemingly endless supply of possible outfits. She flat out refused any skirts or dresses, she had enough of those and just wanted to wear pants for a while. She found 3 pairs of pants that she really liked and a couple cardigans and suit jackets. She made sure the jackets she picked out would match the pants. Next Lacey led her to a shoe store.

Lacey tried on the most ridiculous heels Jane had ever seen.

"I will never understand you and heels" Jane laughed.

"That's because you're not vertically challenged babe" she retorted.

Jane had plenty of shoes, already, that would work with the stuff she bought. Lacey decided against the shoes saying that if there was nothing else she liked better, anywhere else, she would get them on her way out. They paused shopping and ate some lunch. Lacey was pleased to see Jane eat her whole sandwich and finish a chocolate milkshake. After lunch they headed to another clothing store this time on the hunt for shirts that would go with the stuff Jane had already gotten.

She found a couple of simple short sleeved sweaters and picked out three different colors. There must be something to that whole retail therapy concept. The further into the day, the better she was feeling, it helped that Lacey was in full blown cheer up mode. She wondered what she would do when Lacey moved to New York. Pushing that thought from her mind, she did her best to try and cheer up.

While they were standing at the register as Lacey was paying for the shoes they saw earlier, Jane said "I want to get my hair cut."

Lacey looked at her shocked and then grinning said "Let's do this."

Walking over to the salon, Lacey asked Jane how short she wanted to cut it.

"Short" was all Jane said in response.

As they waited, they flipped through style books. Jane finally settled on a cute layered bob. It was a big departure from her long brown hair. All she could think was Wyatt would have hated it, and that was reason enough to do it.

Lacey gave her multiple opportunities to change her mind, and for them to leave, but Jane was adamant.

Lacey tried her best not to hover as Jane's haircut began. Jane closed her eyes and did her best to relax as her hair was being cut. She could almost psychologically feel the weight being lifted from her scalp. She also kept her eyes closed because she did not want to see all of her hair now on the floor. She peeked while the stylist was blow drying her hair but she was not pointed in the direction of a mirror so she gave up and just closed her eyes again.

Once her hair was done, and she was centered on the mirror she opened her eyes. She hardly recognized herself. Her hair felt so soft and full of body. She shook her head feeling her hair tickle her nose. She could not stop touching it and fluffing it. The cut was very flattering, framing her face. She turned to Lacey, who was clasping her hands to her chest ready to jump up and down with excitement. Jane could not wait for her parents to see.

"Alright now let's go get tattoos."Lacey joked.

Jane was feeling better than she had in a long time.

"Thank you for being there for me" she told Lacey suddenly serious.

"No worries, I got you, babe" Lacey said pulling out of the mall.

When they entered Jane's house her mother called out from the den

"Come here I want to see what you got." When Jane walked into the room she cried "What did you do to your hair?"

"Do you like it?" Jane asked twirling.

"It's just so short" she said getting up and coming to get a close look. "It's very cute, but such a surprise."

While Jane showed her mother the clothes she purchased, she would catch her staring at her now much shorter hair. Her mother loved what she had picked out and thought Lacey's shoes were crazy but very Lacey.

When her father got home, he took one look at her and told her the cut "Suited her."

He then quickly collected his credit card winking at her. Lacey headed home after promising to spend the next day at the pool with Jane. Her parents were pleasantly surprised when Jane offered to make them dinner. Jane was not as good of a cook as her mother. She prepared a simple chicken and rice dish she found on the back of a can of soup.

She ate seconds to the relief of Mr. and Mrs. Martin. That night she fell asleep without crying. Did she cry over Wyatt at any point after that day? Yes. Was she as miserable as she had been before? No. The next two weeks, she thankfully did not hear back from the temp agency and filled her time hanging out with Lacey. When Lacey moved she would only have one more week of freedom before starting her job.

She spent much of the next two weeks with Lacey. She helped her pack and sell the furniture that she was not taking with her. With the exception of a cool dresser she got second hand that the Martins would store for her in their spare bedroom indefinitely. Otherwise they hung out at the pool and Lacey did her best to try and get Jane drawing again. It wasn't as though her thoughts would drift directly to Wyatt anymore, she just didn't feel like it.

She was finding happiness in unexpected places, though. She talked her parents into letting her get a cat. The way allergy medications were now, her mother could tolerate the kitten since Jane found a short haired breed. Her kitten was a rescue and Jane named him Ronald after the red hair kid from the Harry Potter movies because he was orange. Daily she found herself laughing out loud at Ronald's high jinks.

Lacey's moving day had come. It was New York or bust. Jane gave Lacey a bear hug and said "Thank you for everything, Lace. Go get them."

"Call me, text me, email me, if you need me I am here for you even from NY" Lacey returned. "Also send me lots of pictures of my godkitty" Lacey added.

Jane stood and waved as she watched her drive away. She brushed a tear off of her cheek and drove home. In only one week she would start her new job. Her first week would be spent shadowing Mr. Hamilton's retiring assistant. Learning how to do her new job. She spent her last week playing with Ronald and further organizing her room. Her mother had all of her new clothes dry cleaned.

Jane would try on different looks in the mirror, trying to find just the perfect outfit for her first day of work. She also was still testing different styles with her new hairdo, as well. Why was it that hair never looked as good as the day you got a haircut she wondered. Plus, she was finding short hair seemed to take more effort than swooping her once long hair in a low ponytail.

When the first came, she went with her new beige pants, a white button up topped with a navy blazer and paired with brown suede flats. Ruth, the assistant she was replacing, was a sweetheart and Jane a fast learner. The work was simple enough. She was in charge of answering the phone and maintaining Mr. Hamilton's calendar. Mr. Hamilton would then request the completion of various forms for his client meetings. When possible, she would pre fill the forms with client information they already had on file.

Mr. Hamilton had a steady stream of business and was particularly busy from January through April 15th for tax season and then again around October, which was just around the corner due to client's who had filed for tax extensions. Jane felt very grown up setting up her direct deposit for her paychecks and selecting her withholdings. It helped that her boss was an accountant.

Jane was very nervous at first on the phone, the computer stuff was no problem but talking to strangers was something else all together. From time to time she would stammer, if she was not sure how to pronounce someone's name. Luckily, must of the calls were inbound and they would say their name for her. By the end of the week, Ruth was confident that she was leaving the reins in capable hands. Jane, on the other hand, was exhausted. Her stretch of unemployment before this job had not prepared her for being on for 8 hours straight.

She would come home play with Ronald, text Lacey, eat dinner then go to bed. She slept in on Saturday and woke up to Ronald batting at her bangs. She opened one eye first, squinting at the little ball of fur on her chest. With her other eye opened, she glanced at her alarm clock. Ugh, earlier than she had hoped but how could she be upset at such a cute kitty. Sitting up, she rubbed her eyes and yawned.

Stepping into her slippers, she padded towards the kitchen with Ronald in her arms. Setting him down by his dish, she added some more kibble and watched him dive into it. Seeing coffee in the pot, she helped herself to a cup and added some French vanilla creamer. Sipping, she watched Ronald eat. Once he was done she made herself a waffle and alternated between taking a bite and pulling a string for Ronald to chase after.

Her dad joined her and they both laughed as Ronald followed Mrs. Martin down the hall batting at her slippers, each step she took.

"I am going to miss that cat when you move out, Janey" her dad said cutting up a cantaloupe.

"We're not going anywhere soon" Jane said reminding him of their three month deal.

She had not even gotten paid yet. Mr. Hamilton paid every two weeks and it turned out she started on the wrong one.

Chapter Twenty-One

J ane had originally agreed to wait three months before she started looking for a place of her own. It had been five. At dinner one evening her father brought the subject up

"How's the apartment search coming, Janey?"

She scrunched her nose and made a noncommittal hmm noise. Her father pressed further and she finally admitted she was delaying her move until she knew for sure what Lacey was doing. Lacey had been living in New York, trying to jumpstart her acting career. They were emailing daily and Jane was sure that Lacey was unhappy there. How do you tell your best friend to give up her dream and move back home? Satisfied Jane was not becoming too comfortable living at home he let it go.

Until then Jane was living in a home and eating food that she did not have to pay for. Her bank account was flush, depending on where she moved, she may even be able to pay an entire years worth of rent up front. Her father was happy to help but wanted to do what he could to make sure they weren't enabling her.

Two months later as Jane had predicted, Lacey confessed that New York was not for her. She was going to move back to Richmond. Jane was thrilled. Once Lacey was back they would find a place together. Lacey stayed with the Martin's while she and Jane looked for a place. She had a heart to heart with Jane that since she didn't have a job yet she was scared it might be better for her to move back in with her folks in Iowa.

Jane was not having that. Lacey had basically been her sole source of comfort, with the exception of Ronald during her rocky breakup. If there were times when Lacey was short, Jane assured her that she had her back. Lacey couldn't argue with that. They were looking for a roomy two bedroom that allowed cats.

They found a place pretty centrally located and jumped on it. It was a two story townhouse style apartment. The doorway opened into a small space with enough room for a table to drop keys off at, and the stairs leading to the main bathroom and bedrooms. It then opened to a living dining space, with the kitchen behind a short wall just past it. The kitchen had another door that led to a back half stair going outside to where their garbage went.

Lacey was thrilled that she had left her funky dresser with the Martin's, because it fit perfectly in her new room. Both she and Lacey needed mattresses but Lacey's parent sprung for the cost of 2 queen sized sets, at a buy one get one sale. The girls considered painting their space but didn't want to have to repaint it when they moved out. They covered the bare white walls with large pieces of art. The painting Lacey's mom had done of the two of them hanging over the sofa the Martin's gave them.

In the beginning, their place was pretty sparse but even the largest space can fill up over time. Lacey was working for the theatre troop she had previously worked with. Their next production was a children's show, so she would be looking for another gig shortly. Their rent was reasonable and their main joint expenses, other than that, were cable, heat, water and groceries, plus they each had a cell phone.

Ronald was the king of the castle. Over time they had acquired a type of scratching post or playhouse in every room. Not that he ever used any of them. More often than not, he would only glance at the one in the living room before curling up in his favorite spot, a perch on the back of the coach. It was close enough to the front window that he could watch the comings and goings of their neighbors.

Lacey eventually ended up working for the same temp agency Jane had worked for, before their road trip. She had not found anything long term yet but when her shifts were early and not on the weekends she and sometimes Jane would still help out on whatever show the theatre was currently running. At least twice a month, they would go have dinner at the Martin's house. They would go more often but they didn't want to annoy Jane's parents and Jane's mom was such a good cook so they kept it at twice a month.

Jane slowly over time began sketching again. It began unexpectedly. She would be writing a list and think Ronald looked so cute peering out their front window, that with her pen, and using the same paper she had, she drew a cute doodle of him. The next time she saw the evening light coming in from the window, in her room, and throwing shadows of a faux birdcage she had on her dresser onto the opposite wall. She took her sketch pad from out of a box on her closet and with a pencil caught the image. It was a wash of the vertical lines of the bird-cage framed by the grid pattern of the window.

She branched out back into the world of pastels and

paint in baby steps. She found a cool old picture frame, at a flea market and painted it hot pink to give to Lacey. She otherwise was a homebody. Lacey dated quite a bit and had been mainly unsuccessful in getting Jane to go on any double dates.

Flipping through a gossip magazine, one day, Jane saw a familiar face. It was an engagement announcement of a Blythe Carlisle to an English footballer. It had been over two years since she had seen Wyatt in Chicago. Jane couldn't help but wonder what he was up to at that moment. She wondered how long he had been split up with Blythe. She also couldn't help but wonder how pissed he probably was that she was getting press and it had nothing to do with him.

She showed Lacey the magazine clipping when she got home from work.

"This was the girl in Chicago?" she asked.

Jane nodded chewing on her lip.

"You are so much prettier than her. Ha! This article said her father friggin owns a broadcasting company. No wonder Wyatt was dating her." Seeing that Jane was looking contemplative, Lacey said "Hey let's get out of here."

"Ahhh" was all Jane could come up with.

"Come on, its wicked hot out there" she said in her best Boston accent "Grab you suit, let's go to your parent's pool." Jane couldn't really argue with that so in no time they were sunbathing. She had a new book, she started reading and zoned out while Lacey flirted with some guys sitting near them. Turns out they were going to be using the pool's barbeque to cook up some burgers and invited them to join them.

Not the type to turn down free food from cute boys,

Lacey readily accepted. Jane being polite put her book away and went to stand with Lacey, as she socialized. After standing there in the hot sun for a couple of minutes, Jane felt really uncomfortable and went to take a dip. Following her lead the group moved to the pool leaving one grumpy fella over a hot grill.

Burgers did not take long to cook though and once they were ready, Lacey helped gather all of the fixings and some side and bring them to a picnic table. As Jane was preparing her burger, she got into a conversation on art stuff with someone named Jim. He went on and on about upcoming shows at their local Fine Art Museum, and how cool the exhibit of Picasso had been. If fact they were the only museum on the east coast that exhibit had come to.

What a coup Jane thought. It was very cool that her home town was becoming so hip on the art scene. It made her also think that she had become very complacent in her current situation. After speaking a bit more and finishing her food, she did a web search on her phone for local museums and galleries.

When she had first graduated, there were two main Art museums in Richmond, and that had not changed, but there were maybe double the galleries she had originally been aware of. She had no interest in quitting her current job, because she had to admit it was a sweet gig. She had very flexible hours, as long as there wasn't a client meeting scheduled, and they were only crazy busy twice a year. She did however have pretty open weekends.

Why hadn't she even considered being a tour guide at one of the museums in town? Poolside, she navigated to the career page of each website. Nothing currently listed but they each had weekend hours so tomorrow she would go and check it out. When Lacey came back to her seat Jane filled her in on her plans for the next day. Lacey could not remember the last time she had seen Jane this excited about something.

Lacey exchanged numbers with one of the boys from the pool and then they returned to their apartment. Jane and Lacey each took a quick shower to rinse the chlorine from their hair. All of that sun really wiped Jane out, she tried to stay awake to watch a movie with Lacey, but gave up and scooping Ronald into her arms on the way went to bed.

The next morning she woke up really hopeful to see what she would learn on her trip downtown. She had some cereal and coffee for breakfast and dressed in a smart black jersey wrap dress with the turquoise necklace and earrings, she had bought when they were in Santa Fe. Lacey was just waking up, as she was walking out the door. As she pulled on some strappy sandals, Lacey wished her luck.

Unfortunately, she had assumed the Sunday hours were the same as the Saturday hours and had to wait around for a hour before either place was open. One museum was also a part of her University. Hoping her alum status might help grease any wheels, she went there first. She was able to find a very helpful tour guide who detailed the various positions that were employed there and what their responsibilities were. She also mentioned that there were various additional people working on site on grant projects.

Grant projects! Jane could have slapped her own forehead. Why hadn't she even thought about submitting a grant proposal? She could easily keep her current job to pay the bills and maybe do research on the side. Plus, if it was her own grant as long as she remained within the parameters of the agreement she would basically be her own boss. This was something she would absolutely need to research further.

She thanked the woman profusely, and then went on to

the other museum. This was the one that hosted the Picasso exhibit. She spoke to someone at information, who was clearly interested in anything other than talking to her. Rude, Jane thought to herself. She could probably do this job better herself. That being said, she was able to discern that they may have a lot of openings prior new exhibits. It even seemed as though there would be flexible night and or weekend hours. She thanked the woman for her help and then went to a nearby gallery.

She had never really checked out a gallery before. This one was very posh. She felt a bit under dressed just walking in. A clerk greeted her and explained the current showing they had. He also gave her a brochure that detailed future shows. Walk ins during the day were free of charge. There was however a nominal fee to attend the first two evening showings of an artist. Not unlike a cover charge to a club.

Unfortunately a gallery did not require an extensive staff as items available for purchase were normally not of a large inventory. Most galleries were either of a sole owner-ship or partnership type. He had gotten his job because the owner was his mother's godfather. He did however seem very interested in seeing some of her work. "We are always on the lookout for local artists" he explained.

Always ready to self deprecate Jane replied "Oh I'm really not any good."

"Might be interesting either way" he said giving her his card. She let him know she would think about it and then left.

Lacey was chopping up vegetables in the kitchen when she returned.

"What's going on here?" she asked looking around, as neither of them were great cooks.

"I got sucked into the cooking channel" Lacey explained. "They made this one pot dish that made me so hungry I had to run to the store, get all the ingredients and try it."

Jane confessed she was starved and ate a string cheese while Lacey prepared her masterpiece.

"I was hoping I would have had it in the oven before you got home but it turns out chopping potatoes takes forever."

Jane told her all about her day and Lacey jumped all over the opportunity for someone to look at her work.

"Jane your work is amazing, especially all of your drawings of Ron."

At the sound of his name Ronald gently padded into the kitchen and wove himself through Lacey's legs a couple times before she had to shoo him away because it tickled. Looking offended he visited his water dish.

"Jane you know people go ape shit over cat stuff" Lacey went on.

"Even if anyone would be interested in buying any of my work, I think I would go crazy not having them. Like as if I was selling my babies" Jane grimaced.

"That is crazy, Jane. Go make money and become rich and famous, then hire me to be your personal assistant" she added with a wink.

All of her chopping done she put water then a can of cream of mushroom soup on a large pot and stirred it. She added potatoes, carrots and celery and again stirred. After placing a large beef roast on top and covering with foil she placed in the oven.

"Holy crap, Lacey, that thing will feed us all week" Jane exclaimed.

"It was the smallest one I could find" Lacey said shrugging, then set the timer for four hours on the oven.

The roast turned out amazing, and the girls did enjoy it two more times that week. The last serving tasted a bit chewy. It was the following weekend that the girls went out Friday night and met Gabe and his friends. Thinking back on all of this, what Jane had not expected was running into Wyatt again, let alone so recently after reading about his now ex girlfriend's engagement. Seemed rather odd and she did not believe in coincidences.

Chapter Twenty-Two

"Hello Wyatt, in town for a visit?" Jane said quietly.

"I've just moved back, I will be beginning an internship with a firm downtown next week" He replied.

Lacey sat in a wing chair and abnormally silent, watched the exchange like a spectator at a tennis match. It turns out Wyatt had stopped by, to leave his new contact information with Jane's mom, to pass along to her, assuming her parents still lived there. After some time he stood, excusing himself as he still had quite a bit of unpacking to do.

"Jane, I would love to get together some time to catch up" He said getting up. Jane's mother looked thrilled "Mrs. Martin, Lacey it was a pleasure to see you both."

"Jane, why don't you walk Wyatt out" Her mother said motioning her to follow him.

She nodded and followed him to the door.

"I am truly sorry, I surprised you" he began "I only meant to drop off my number but your mom..."

"No" Jane interrupted "it's fine, don't apologize."

He gave her a stiff hug and then was gone.

Jane shut the door then leaned against it, in an attempt to let her brain process what had just happened.

"Jane!" her mother called from the living room, snapping her back to reality.

"Coming, mom" Lacey was giving her a 'holy crap did that just really happen' look when she reentered the room.

"Wasn't that a lovely surprise" Mrs. Martin gushed, smoothing her sweater "Pity you weren't more presentable. When I opened the door, well, you could have pushed me down with a feather, when I saw Wyatt. What s nice young man, and an internship downtown, how impressive."

"Alright mom, where's your camera?" Jane said happy to change the subject.

Jane got through her lesson as fast as possible, Lacey and Mr. Martin shared a pitcher of lemonade as he watched the golf channel. After promising her mom she would call and let her know when she heard from Wyatt, and then kissing her dad on the cheek she and Lacey bolted.

Once in the car Lacey said "Oh my god, what are you thinking?"

"I have no idea what just happened" Jane replied "I mean I was there but I just don't think my brain believes it. I just figured once we broke up that was it. I would probably never see him again. I am really surprised, he is doing an internship here. I just figured he would want to be in a bigger city. And stopping by my parent's house, kinda weird right? And could I have looked worse?" Jane went on.

"Hush you look adorable" Lacey objected.

"Thanks, babe, it's just not a look I would chose to run into an ex in." Jane replied. Bzzz bzzz bzz "Hey Lace, grab my cell, I think it's buzzing."

Lacey pulled Jane' smart phone from her purse and confirmed "Yep, looks like a text. Want me to read it?"

Jane nodded.

"Hi Jane, its Gabe from last night…" Lacey read. Jane's mouth dropped open and Lacey squealed.

"Keep reading!" Jane pleaded.

"I wanted to know if you would like to go out, sometime. How is your schedule this week?" Now, it was Jane's turn to squeal. "Wow, he's texting you the next day. He must really like you" Lacey said.

Jane grinned and did a little shimmy in her seat.

"Do you want me to reply?" Lacey asked with a mischievous glint in her eyes.

"Do and die!" Jane replied laughing.

They pulled up to their apartment. Jane was stressing over how to respond, without coming off over eager. Hey Gabe, sounds rad! – Jane………eww no. 'Hi Gabe, I would love to get together. Love Jane'…....too strong. 'Gabe, yes. Jane'…… probably too short. This is hard Jane thought. She finally settled with "Hi Gabe, that sounds fun. When were you thinking?" Send.

Then Jane began stalking her messages status to see if he responded. Jane and Lacey both jumped when her phone rang.

"Is that Gabe? Lacey asked.

"I don't know, I don't recognize the number" Jane said. She shrugged her shoulders and answered "Hello?....Oh hi, Wyatt."

Lacey's mouth dropped open. Jane waved her off and walked into the kitchen. She spoke to him for a couple of minutes and then said good bye and came back into the living room.

"Soooooooooo……" Lacey began "Did you give Wyatt your number earlier?"

"Nope" Jane replied "my mother gave it to him."

"What did he want?" Lacey encouraged.

"He wanted to see if I would meet him for coffee" Jane said looking at her feet.

"hmmm" was all Lacey said in response.

"It's no big deal" Jane started feeling defensive "just coffee."

Lacey kept her lips firmly shut and nodded.

Jane humpfed and threw a sofa pillow at her, which startled Ronald causing him to levitate and cracked her up.

"Alright, alright" Lacey began "Just don't turn into a pod person, this time."

Jane nodded, she was still processing the recent events. Ronald gave them both what only could be described as a withering glare, and went upstairs.

"Look, Lace" Jane began after composing herself "I really do not know what Wyatt's motive is for reaching out to me. He may just want to be friends"

At this Lacey started mock banging her head on the coffee table.

"Thing is" Jane continued pointedly ignoring her, "I have no interest in getting back together with Wyatt."

Lacey smiled at this but still did not look convinced. "So, why are you going?" Lacey countered.

"Honestly, I'm curious" Jane said "he was a big part of my life."

Lacey rolled her eyes and changing the subject said "Did Gabe text back?"

Jane jumped for her phone "Let me check. He did! It says 'Sweet, how does Wednesday sound?' "That's so far away" Jane pouted.

"Oh hush, dork" Lacey laughed "it's only 4 days away."

"Alright, alright" Jane smiled. "It'll give me time to get

my nails done. Should I meet him out or let him pick me up here?"

"What scared, he's a mass murderer posing as a middle school teacher?" Lacey grinned "What's his last name? Let's Google him"

"Really? Do you think that would be anything out there?" Jane asked "I feel like this is invading his privacy."

Lacey was not going to be put off. Opening her lap top she demanded "Last name!"

"Fine! Dixon." Jane said sitting down next to her on the sofa and watching Lacey enter his name into the search engine.

"Probably not the musician, or the plumber." Lacey laughed. "There seem to be a lot people named Gabe Dixon. She re-entered the search including city and state. "I think we have a hit there's an article about a local teacher…blah blah a local teacher Gabe Dixon received a commendation with his class for surpassing a fundraising goal for a local charity. There's a picture!"

Jane grabbed the laptop from Lacey. "How cute! It's him with his class."

"Yes, very cute. Grabby mcgrab-grab!" Lacey fussed at her "I think it's safe to let him pick you up here."

Jane texted him back her info and a confirmation that Wednesday night would work.

"I'm so bummed, I didn't meet a yummy guy too" Lacey pouted.

"Didn't you think Gabe's friend Matt was cute?" Jane asked.

"I guess, but he didn't ask for my number so what does it matter?"

"Do you want me to get it from Gabe?" Jane questioned.

"Oh hell no, I am not desperate. So what's the game plan for tonight?" Lacey asked hopefully.

"No way, we were out way too late last night. I am taking it easy for the rest of the weekend" Jane replied.

"Boo! I wanna meet a boy" Lacey whined.

"Plus I have to meet Wyatt for coffee tomorrow" Jane said.

"Ugh, come on P.L.E.A.S.E........." Lacey hugged Jane's arm and gave made her best impression of a pitiful look which came off looking more constipated than anything else.

Either way it worked, Jane laughed and said "Fine, but only two drinks."

Lacey jumped up yelling "I love you, I love you, and I'm hitting the shower first" and dashed out of the room.

"Don't use all of the hot water" Jane called after her.

She walked into the kitchen and grabbed a bag of chips. Then sat down in the living room. She shook her head trying to wrap her brain around the last 24 hours. Plans with 2 guys in the next week, crazy she thought.

"All yours" Lacey shouted from the hallway.

Jane showered and threw on a cute top and jeans. Lacey got decked out in a short skirt, sequined top and boots.

"So where are we going?" Jane asked.

"No jeans!" Lacey replied "get your cute butt back into your room and change"

"Ugh, come on I want to wear jeans" Jane grumbled

"If you must…" Lacey said scrunching her nose.

"Yes, I must" Jane confirmed "And since we are not staying out all night again let's move it" and propelled Lacey to the door.

"Ok, tonight's mission is to find me a hottie" Lacey grinned.

"Wanna go to a sports bar? Lots of boys there" Jane asked.

"Great idea. Let's go!"

They headed to a popular local bar. There must have been a big game on because the place was packed. They made their way inside and learned their college team was playing.

"Sweet!" Jane said and they grabbed a table and ordered drinks.

They were definitely getting checked up by some guys but since the game was close, that was getting more attention than Lacey wanted.

"This blows, when's halftime?" Lacey moaned.

"Hush, it's soon. Look at the screen there are only like 2 min left." Jane replied.

At halftime a couple of guys came over. "So, who are you cheering for?" one asked.

"Rams all the way" Lacey grinned "we both went there."

"Hey stranger" Jane heard behind her. She turned,

"No way!" she smiled "Hey Gabe."

He gave her a big hug and gave the guy who was standing on the other side of her a 'move along' look. Jane felt her heart race, feeling his arms around her. He felt fit and warm or maybe that was her because Lord it suddenly felt hot in there. They both laughed when they realized the hug should probably be over by now. Jane blushed and smiled up at him.

"Are you following me?" Gabe teased.

"Nope, we got here first" Jane countered.

"Nope, I've been here for awhile" Gabe smiled "And I definitely would have noticed if you were here. Come on, there is a whole group of us sitting over there."

Jane looked at Lacey.

"Sure" Lacey said picking up their drinks.

Gabe took Jane's hand (!!!!!!!!!!!!) and led her to his table with Lacey following. Once there they recognized a couple of guys from previous evening.

"So you went to VCU?" Gabe asked as they sat.

"Yep, where did you go?" Jane replied. Gabe pointed to the opposing team.

"Mason? No way, we're rivals. I may have to cancel our date" Jane joked.

"Oh, I see how it is. How about a friendly wager?"

What did you have in mind?" Jane asked.

He mischievously rubbed his hands together. "Loser bakes winner dinner tomorrow night?"

"Deal, but I'm a terrible cook"

"It's okay, I'll take my chances."

At this point Gabe's friend Matt walked over.

"Hey Jane! Gabe has been talking about you nonstop since last night"

Jane looked up at Gabe who looked pretty red and punched Matt in the shoulder.

"Thanks Matt, anything else you want to embarrass me with?"

"Where to start?" Matt smiled.

"Matt was just leaving" Gabe said pushing him towards the other end of the table. Gabe turned back to Jane grimacing "He loves to give me a hard time."

Jane laughed "It was pretty funny, you got pretty red, plus you didn't even notice that 3 pointer. I'm wondering what you'll be cooking me for dinner."

"I'm picking up a competitive vibe here. So, on the off chance you win. What would you like for dinner?" Gabe asked.

"Oh anything would be fine" Jane said blushing.

At that they turned and watched the game. Jane kept

sneaking glances at Gabe. The lighting was so much better here than the previous night. He was really cute. He was about 6 ft tall and had a solid lanky build. He had short brown hair that sat in a carefree style. Not too much gel if any. He had a scruffy 3 o'clock shadow, so she guessed he had not shaved today.

He was wearing hiking sneakers, dark wash jeans and a black polo. She went to sneak another peek and caught him doing the same thing. She looked away quickly and bit her lip. Gabe chuckled and cleared his throat. Jane met his eyes trying her best innocent expression. They both started laughing.

"So" Gabe said catching his breath "Can I get you another one?" and gestured towards her drink.

"Sure!" Lacey boomed draping her arm around Jane "I'd love another, get one for Jane too while you're at it."

"Lacey" Jane admonished.

"It's cool Jane, I'll be right back" Gabe smiled and headed towards the bar.

"Some pretty good looking guys here tonight" Lacey said sitting down. "It is crazy that we ran into Gabe, I think you are going to owe me big time sista."

"Guess what" Jane gushed "we have a bet going on the game. Loser makes dinner tomorrow night. That means we'll be seeing each other three nights in a row!"

"Yikes, do I need to be looking for a new roommate?" Lacey joked.

"Shut up, it's just really exciting right now" Jane replied.

"Shh, he's coming back" Lacey whispered.

Gabe set the drinks down and Lacey grabbed hers and blew him a kiss and headed towards a group of guys playing a golf arcade game.

"Oh, watch this" Jane said pointing towards Lacey

"she is a total, well whatever the equivalent of a pool shark for this game."

The guys had parted to let Lacey have a turn. She set down her drink and very daintily crushed all of their high scores. A collective "Whoa" rose from the group.

"Ahh, thanks guys" Lacey said as she picked her drink back up patted one guy on the stomach and headed back towards Jane.

Someone in the group called out "Best 2 out of 3?" Lacey winked at Jane and turned around. Jane turned back to Gabe laughing and raised her brow at him as he seemed to appraise her.

"Yes?" she asked.

""You two seem very different to be friends" he said.

"It's always been like that" Jane began "We met freshman year. We shared a dorm and the rest is history. I've always been a bit shy and Lacey doesn't have a shy bone in her body. We kinda balance each other out. She gets me out of my shell and I help her embrace moderation. Speaking of moderation, we were supposed to leave one drink ago but I can't miss how the game ends now"

"Looks like I'm up" Gabe said tapping the table.

"Not for long" Jane teased.

"So, I never asked what you went to school for" Gabe replied "You work for an accountant, right?"

She nodded

"Did you study business?"

"Nope, I was an Art History major" Jane grimaced. "Maybe someday I'll work in a museum, but until then I'm just happy to pay the bills."

"Very cool" Gabe said "I took some art history classes in college and seeing as how I ended up a History teacher I am a fan."

A large whoop sounded all around them, as Jane's team took the lead.

"Not looking good for you" Jane whispered in Gabe's ear.

Before she sat back up he turned his face towards hers. With their noses almost touching Jane held her breath as Gabe looked deeply into her eyes.

After a long pause he returned "Want to hear a secret?"

Incapable of speech at that moment Jane nodded.

Gabe quietly said "I win either way." Then smiled and turned his head back to the game.

Jane a slight shade of red, felt her heart pounding in her chest and slowly straightened. Oh my lord, she thought, and suddenly could not wait until tomorrow night. Her mind was so preoccupied she completely missed the final minutes of the game.

"Looks like I'm cooking" Gabe smiled "Any special requests? Also, any chance I can cook at your place? When I mentioned I had no AC that was just brushing the surface."

"Of course" Jane began "I can help"

Gabe interrupted "No way, you won. I'll cook and clean."

"Alright, alright" Jane laughed "You can wait on me hand and foot."

She turned and caught sight of Lacey and some guy looking very occupied in a corner of the bar.

She gestured towards her "I should probably go get her."

"That sounds fun, can I watch?" Matt called out from down the table. Gabe rolled his eyes.

Jane shook her head and went to collect Lacey which turned out to be easier said than done. At first Mr. Romeo said that he was going home with them. Jane quickly put an end to that idea while Lacey pouted. They settled on exchanging info and sharing one last very long and not PG kiss. Jane's eyes met Gabe's across the bar and she glanced at Lacey and her 'friend' than back at Gabe and shrugged.

They met up with Gabe and all headed towards the parking lot together. Jane unlocked her car and Lacey yawning loudly climbed in. Jane lingered by her car door for Gabe to do something.

"Are you alright to drive?" Gabe asked "I can follow you if you'd like."

"I'm good, just tired" Jane replied.

"Okay" Gabe said "Is 5 o'clock good for tomorrow?" he went on.

"Sounds good" she said opening her door and getting in her car.

"Hey Jane"

She popped back up

"I am really looking forward to seeing you tomorrow" Gabe said and leaned in to place a soft kiss on her cheek and with a wave headed to his car.

Her hand rose to the spot his lips just were. It felt warm. She watched him get into his car and with a small wave headed home. She could not wait. And had a cheek aching grin the whole drive home, while she unlocked her apartment door and until she sat down on the sofa. She knew she had to sleep but was way too excited to do anything but replay that kiss over and over again in her mind.

She finally snapped out of it, when Lacey said "Hey I missed what happened with your bet, who won?"

"I did" Jane replied "He wants to cook over here. Any chance I can have the place to myself, tomorrow night?"

"I'm not sleeping someplace else but I can make myself scarce. So why is he cooking over here?" Lacey replied.

"I guess his kitchen is a mess" Jane murmured "he said something about having a fixer upper house."

"He owns his own house!" Lacey boomed "Very grown up. Bummer it's not all done yet. So are you going cancel your coffee thing tomorrow?"

"Oh CRAP!" Jane exclaimed "I had completely forgotten about it."

"So, what are you going to do?" Lacey asked.

"I don't know, what should I do?" Jane worried "I mean it's just coffee…"

"Right" Lacey replied "How long can that take, let an hour?"

"Your right, Lace, besides all I have to do is pick up a little and get ready before Gabe comes. Will you help me speed clean in the morning?" Jane pleaded.

"Sure, babe, I'll help but now bed" Lacey grumbled heading towards her room.

Jane washed her makeup off, brushed her teeth changed into some old sweats and a t shirt, she was out as soon as her head touched the pillow.

Chapter Twenty-Three

The beeping of a truck backing up woke her the next morning. She rubbed her eyes and glanced at the clock, 9am.

"Darn" she grimaced getting up.

She had hoped it was earlier so she could sleep in a bit longer. She headed to the kitchen to make some coffee. Lacey stumbled in and Jane raised her brow at her.

"Don't judge" Lacey grumbled "I'm still waking up. Coffee ready?" and sat on a stool.

"Almost" Jan replied as she took out 2 mugs "How do you want it?"

"Black as my soul" Lacey could be dramatic at times. Jane handed her a steaming mug "I love you the mostest!" Lacey trilled "So what do you want me to clean?" Lacey asked between sips.

"You pick" Jane said "we need to take out the trash, and straighten and wipe down the bathroom and kitchen. Maybe pick up here and there. Other than that I think I'll burn a vanilla candle so it smells good. So, trash or kitchen and bath?"

"I call trash" Lacey said "then I'll take a shower."

"So what are you going to do while Gabe is over; meet up with your friend from last night?" Jane asked

"Hmm, I think I'll let him come to me" Lacey winked.

"So tell me what happened while I pick up the bathroom" Jane said heading down the hall pulling Lacey after her.

Lacey sat on the edge of the tub while Jane took stuff of the counter and placed them into the cabinet below the sink.

"Did you lure him in with your golf skills?" Jane joked sprit zing the counter with cleanser.

"Kinda" Lacey snorted "He was the only one brave enough to challenge me. There was no why he was going to beat me but he was pretty cute trying. We got to talking after and I guess I just grabbed his face and started kissing him. I don't think he minded."

"I'll bet!" Jane laughed "He seemed very happy and got your number."

Lacey shrugged her shoulders sheepishly. Jane wiped down the toilet and motioned for Lacey to move so she could wipe down the tub.

"Do you think he's going to shower here?" Lacey teased wagging her brows at Jane.

"Of course not" Jane huffed "but he might look behind the curtain."

"Why would he look behind the curtain?" Lacey snorted.

"Better safe than sorry" Jane scrunched her nose.

"If you want to be better safe than sorry you should change your sheets and stock up on protection" Lacey snickered.

Jane blushed and mumbled something incoherently as Lacey laughed. Together they headed back to the living room and each had a bowl of cereal. Jane took both bowls when they were finished and placed them in the sink then headed to take a shower. She struggled with what to wear.

She wanted to look nice but she didn't want to look like she was trying to look nice. It was strange normally she got dressed just trying to look pretty and comfortable given whatever kind of weather was going on. But, in this situation she both wanted to look good to make Wyatt regret how things ended but at the same time not good enough for him to think she was interested in him. It was a conundrum.

She went with dark washed jeans and long sleeved black shirt and ballet flats. He preferred her hair down so she purposefully wore it in a low pony tail. She kept her makeup simple and used a light floral body spray, brushed her teeth, applied lip gloss and headed out. Lacey called out as she reached the door

"Ahh, I was hoping you would get all decked out and make him rue the day he ever broke up with you."

"Don't be silly Lace; I am wearing exactly what someone meeting an old friend would wear. Besides I would hate for Wyatt to think I was getting dressed up for him" Jane returned "And hey, don't forget the trash."

Jane grabbed her keys and sunglasses and headed out. She stopped for gas on the way, it was a breezy morning. As she stood by the pump she regretted not wearing a light jacket. The weather in Richmond never quite made up its mind during the change of seasons. It was warm one day then almost freezing the next, then warm again.

She contemplated running into the convenience store for some vitamin C but decided against it because she did not want to be late. Before taking off she took out her phone and opened the picture Gabe had sent her of the 2 of them and mentally thought she would definitely get dressed up for their date. Even with her stop she still ended up at the café a couple of minutes early.

Great, she thought Wyatt would probably take this as her being eager to see him. Sometimes her punctuality backfired. A positive though in beating him there was she could order and pay for herself. That way he would not be able to offer and assume they were on a date. She used to hate it when he would order for her, even when she told him what she wanted he would change it every time. It was funny that she remembered that now.

One time he had even ordered skim milk and no sugar coffee instead of her normal cream and sugar while explaining to her it was never too soon to start watching her figure. Grrr, just thinking of that made she order a chocolate croissant with her coffee just to spite him. She had just finished paying when he entered and admonished her

"Jane, you should have waited for me, I would have taken care of this."

She sweetly replied "No worries, I can take care of myself."

Wyatt nodded and went to place his order as Jane found a table flanked with 2 cozy armchairs, outside of the draft range of the entrance.

When he came to sit down he began "Jane it is so good to see you again. We must do this more often."

"Mmm" was all Jane could manage in response. After a few moments of awkward silence Jane said "So, tell me about your internship."

That was all Wyatt needed to launch into a detailed monologue of the absolute honor of receiving such a sought after position with a prominent local engineering firm.

"That is very impressive Wyatt" Jane said trying her best to seem interested.

"I know it's impressive" Wyatt sniffed.

Jane thought to herself he was humble as ever. She did her best not to giggle but looked forward to telling Lacey. Just then she heard.

"Is that you Jane?"

She turned to see Gabe's friend Matt behind her.

"Oh hey Matt, how are you?" Jane replied.

"Aren't you going to introduce me?" Wyatt huffed.

"Of course" Jane said flustered "Matt this Wyatt, Wyatt Matt."

"So Matt, how do you know my girlfriend?" Wyatt asked puffing up his chest.

"Your girlfriend?" Matt repeated looking at Jane.

Jane meanwhile felt frozen place expect for her jaw which dropped as she looked at Wyatt in disbelief.

She composed herself and pointedly said "We used to date, we do not currently date."

That managed to deflate Wyatt only slightly until he looked directly at Matt and replied "For now."

Matt laughed and returned "Huh, that's really interesting seeing as how Jane…"

But, Jane cut him off and said "It was nice seeing you Matt." He gave her an 'are you sure?' look and shrugged when she nodded.

Taking that is a hint he said "Jane, it was nice seeing you" then turning to Wyatt "I'd say the same for you but, well you know I just can't. Bye Jane" and left.

Jane cringed imagining what he would say to Gabe. She turned to Wyatt "Why would you say that?" she exclaimed.

"Jane dear, I assumed that you understood that is where this is going" he returned gesturing around them.

"No, I did not assume a coffee to catch out with an old friend would constitute a rekindling of our relationship" Jane groaned. She picked up her purse and coffee then took a pointedly large final bite of her croissant and headed for the door.

"Jane don't over react" Wyatt called after her.

Jane struggled getting her keys into the ignition of her sedan. Once the car was started she took 5 deep cleansing breaths before shifting into reverse and heading home.

She muttered to herself the whole way home. She alternated between 'what a jerk and holy crap and oh my god'. By the time she got home she may have been more ticked off then she was when she had left the café.

"Lacey!" She called out when she entered the apartment "you will not even believe what just friggin happened."

She slammed her keys and purse down.

Lacey calmly looked up from a fashion magazine "Must be bad, you broke out a friggin."

Jane relayed the café drama while pacing back and forth from the kitchen to the living room.

"No he did not!" Lacey gasped.

"I know, right?" Jane replied miserably "Matt is going to totally tell Gabe. How awkward. Oh my God, what if Gabe cancels?"

Lacey looked pensive and returned "Well, this could actually work in your favor. If Gabe knows other guys are into you maybe he'll up his game."

Jane replied "I don't even want to think about games" and dramatically laid down across the sofa pulling a pillow over her head.

"Alrighty missy, it is not time to turn into a pumpkin cause you have a prince coming to cook for you so let's get you all dolled up."

Lacey changed the TV channel from what she was watching to one of top 40 music stations and blasted it. Singing and dancing around the coffee table she pulled Jane up and followed her with her hands on Jane's hips shimmying her to her room. Lacey's happiness was very contagious and Jane was able shake off her anxiety.

Jane tried on different looks for her dinner date and with Lacey's blessing settled on a sassy blue jersey dress. The front was a bit low cut for Jane but after the day she had she felt like being a little daring. She re-showered and mentally allowed the stress and drama from earlier melt away from her in the hot water. Lacey did her eye makeup for her and earning brownie points a curled her hair too.

When Jane looked in the mirror she giggled

"I feel like I'm going to prom." Lacey grabbed her cell phone and returned "That must be why I feel like taking your picture" she snapped a couple of shots including one with her arm around Jane and their faces smushed together.

"If we had a fireplace mantle, this picture would be hung above it." Lacey said admiring her photographic skills then turned the TV off. "Babe, you look amazing. I'm going to beat feet, heading to the mall to do some serious damage to my credit card." and blew kisses to her on the way out the door.

Chapter Twenty-Four

Jane put on some simple strappy sandals and lit a candle. She took one last look around the apartment before there was a knock at the door. She took a deep breath walked over and checked the peephole. Gabe was standing there with flowers (!) and a brown paper grocery bag. She opened the door smiling.

"Any ex-boyfriends hiding in there" he asked, peeking his head into the doorway.

Jane flushed bright red "How embarrassing, I take it Matt told you we ran into each other today."

Sensing her discomfort Gabe grinned "No worries, if I was ever dumb enough to lose a girl like you I guess I would be trying to get you back as well."

Jane beamed

"So" he continued "Now that that is behind us there is nothing stopping us from having a great night. These are for you" Gabe handed her a beautiful bouquet of lilies.

"Thank you, they are gorgeous" Jane gushed. "Let me put them in a vase."

She closed the door behind Gabe and he followed her

to the kitchen. She pointed out the bathroom on the way. As she set about filling a vase with water he placed the grocery bag on the counter and unloaded its contents.

"This is a nice place" he remarked.

"We like it" Jane returned "we've lived here just over a year."

Jane carried the flowers over to a small bistro table the girls had off the side of their living room. It was small and meant for a patio but worked well as a dinning space in their quaint apartment. Ronald came to investigate him, coiling himself through his legs and smelled Gabe's shoes.

"He must smell my dog" Gabe said as Ronald slowly sniffed his shoes.

"Come on Ronald" Jane said scooping him up "Try to be polite to our guest."

She set him on his favorite perch on the back of the couch. He turned around three times than laid down keeping his eyes on Gabe.

"I'll move the flowers when we eat, but for now they look pretty here" Jane surmised as she played with their arrangement.

"They are not the only pretty things over there" Gabe said pointedly "You look really beautiful."

Jane blushed and looked down feeling very shy "Thank you" she whispered.

Gabe grinned and said "I hope you like chicken cacciatore because if you don't I'm in trouble."

"I love it" Jane replied "Can I help?"

"All I need is a quick tour of where your pots, pans and other cooking type gear is, and of course your company while I cook."

Jane pointed out where they stored their cooking gear, it was limited but thankfully they had what Gabe needed for the meal.

"Should I put on some music?" Jane asked.

"Sure" Gabe replied as he filled a pot with water.

They both jumped when Jane turned on the TV since the volume had not been turned back down from earlier. Jane quickly turned it down and smiled sheepishly at Gabe.

"I thought we were back in the club" he joked.

"Err, sorry. Getting ready music" Jane grimaced.

"No apologies. I do the same thing at home, just more rock than pop."

Jane went with a channel that mainly played hits from the 60s and set it at a comfortable background noise level.

"I wasn't sure if you like wine or not. I brought a bottle of white and of red in case you had a preference. Would you like a glass?" Gabe asked.

"I'd love a glass of red" she replied moving behind him to take down a couple of wine glasses from a cabinet.

The kitchen area was pretty tight for two. As she set the glasses on the counter he turned to face her. She motioned to the drawer he was leaning against and he stepped towards her closing the negative space between them. They locked eyes as she reached behind him to open the drawer and take out a bottle opener. She could feel heat radiating off of him as her hand fumbled around in the drawer.

"It is in here somewhere" she mumbled as their eyes met.

It probably would have helped if she was actually looking in the drawer and not into his eyes. She felt her mouth water, man she could really use that glass of wine. Chuckling he reached his hand into the drawer as well and their hands closed over it at the same time. They stood there frozen and Gabe began to lean his face towards hers when BEEP! They both jumped at the notification ding that the oven was preheated.

"I'll open the wine" Jane breathed heavily and stepped away. Gabe nodded and put the chicken in the oven and the noodles in the pan inwardly cursing the creator of the preheat notification. He set the timer on the stove and Jane handed him a glass of wine

"We have 35 min for the chicken to be done. Want to sit and talk while we wait?" Gabe asked.

"Sounds good" Jane said stepping into the living room.

"So tell me about yourself" Gabe said sitting down.

"Well I was born not far from here and my parents still live in the house I grew up in. In High School I was very shy, got good grades but not into afterschool clubs. I went to VCU for their Art History program. I met Lace our freshman year. After graduation I found out very quickly that I couldn't move out of my parent's house unless I found a paying job. One of my dad's golf buddies set me up with my current job. It pays the bills and I don't have to work weekends so I'm pretty content."

Jane took a deep gulp of her wine and said "Your turn."

Gabe stood as he spoke and moved the flowers from the table to the kitchen counter and began to set the table. "My dad was in the Air Force so we moved around a lot. We lived in Germany for a bit. He is retired now. My folks live in New Hampshire now and spend their winters in Florida. We were living near DC when I was in High School so I ended up going to George Mason."

"I always wanted to be a teacher." He continued "I think it may have come from experiencing so many different ones over the years. I had some awesome teachers but some really rotten ones too. I played soccer through school and still follow the Barclay's league today. I have an older brother, Jake who is in the Air Force and stationed with his family out in Las Vegas now. I have a niece and a nephew; they are a lot of fun when I get to see them. I have a house not far from the bar where we met. It needs a lot of work. I've been tackling one room at a time. So far I have the main level almost done. I'm working on the kitchen right now which is why I asked to borrow yours. It's slow moving because I am doing the work in my spare time. I have a bulldog, Baby. Babe for short, she is a lazy bum but a sweetheart.

At that the oven buzzed and Gabe got up to take the chicken out of the oven and prep the plates. He set the plates on the table and went back to also bring a couple of plates of salad with dressing. They both sat down to eat.

After her first bite Jane gushed "Oh my god, this is really good. Where did you learn to cook?"

Gabe smiled "My mom is an awesome cook, I've got nothing on her but she did teach me a few things."

Once they were both finished Gabe took both of their plates to the sink then rinsed and placed them in the dish-washer. Jane silently thanked Lacey for unloading the dish-washer while she was gone. She went and sat on the sofa and regarded Gabe as he dried his hands on a dish towel. He looked so cute and big in her tiny kitchen.

Gabe refilled their glasses and asked Jane if she would like some chocolate.

"Twist my arm" Jane replied grinning.

He brought a package of really nice dark chocolate from the kitchen.

"Fancy" Jane remarked looking at the package.

"I told you I lived in Germany" he laughed "they don't mess around with chocolate over there."

She selected a chocolate in the shape of a shell, closed her eyes and let it melt on her tongue. Gabe could not take his eyes off of her. She opened her eyes and caught him staring. She raised a brow at him in question.

He cleared his throat and chuckled "You look very sexy eating chocolate."

Wow it got hot in there; she had to resist the urge to fan herself. He selected a piece and plopped it in his mouth. She had to admit he looked pretty good eating it as well. Not sure what to do next Jane took a big swig of her wine. There was a jingling at the door then a booming

"Honey I'm home!" as Lacey entered the apartment. "Ya'll decent?" she called out.

Jane choked out a "Yes"

So Lacey returned "Pity, do you want me to go back out so ya'll can get to business?"

"I'm going to kill you" Jane sweetly replied.

Lacey came into the living room carrying a few shopping bags from the mall.

"Hey Gabe, man it smells good in here. Any chance there are any left over's?" she asked hopefully

Gabe nodded and got up to make her a plate. Their eyes met and Jane shrugged. Lacey went to her room to drop her bags off. Jane went to meet Gabe in the kitchen.

"I'm sorry" she began

"Don't apologize; I needed to take off soon anyways. As you know it is a school night."

"Don't rush off on my account" Lacey replied coming back into the living room.

"No worries" Gabe said as he handed Lacey a plate of food "I have to get back to my dog before she thinks I've abandoned her."

He picked up in the kitchen, leaving Jane the rest of the chocolates.

"I'll walk you out" Jane said getting up.

As they walked out of the room she mimed strangling Lacey. While Lacey, mouthful of food and all mouthed 'Sorry'. Jane grabbed a sweater as she and Gabe walked out together. The cool fall air gave her goose bumps. They walked in silence to Gabe's car. He reached for her hand and his hand felt warm when she placed her hand into it.

"I had a really great time" Gabe said as they approached his car.

"Me too" Jane replied looking at her feet.

"I'm up here Jane" Gabe said placing a finger under her chin and feather light slowly lifted it until their eyes met.

They held each other's gaze for a beat and then he said "Jane, I'd really like to kiss you right now, that okay?"

He held his breath as she signed "Yes."

He brought his lips almost to her and just before she closed her eyes she saw him smile. His lips were soft on hers. They stood like that for a few seconds with his hand under her chin. They pulled back a hair and he dropped his hand to her waist and pulled her back to him for a deeper kiss.

When they both straightened he said "Till Wednesday. I'll pick you up at 7."

"I can't wait" Jane replied feeling light headed from the kiss or the wine or some sort of combination of the two.

She cringed inwardly afterward thinking to herself 'way to play it cool Jane'. He smiled and got into his car. As she began to walk away he started his car and pulled alongside her.

He rolled down his window and said "Goodnight Jane"

She turned and waved and he waited till he had seen her reenter her apartment and then was gone. She floated in the living room where Lacey was just finishing her plate.

Lacey regarded Jane for a moment before declaring "Ya'll totally kissed."

Jane bobbed her head excitedly then twirled in placed and squealed

"We did!" She went on to tell Lacey about her evening.

Lacey was pleased to hear how he had played off the whole Wyatt hub bub and thought the flowers he brought were perfect. She then declared she was willing to let her bestie date him on the condition that he cook frequently.

When Jane offered Lacey one of the chocolates he had brought she inhaled it then very seriously said "Marry him." Jane knew Lacey was only joking but she had to admit Gabe was total boyfriend material. After the girls each enjoyed another chocolate Lacey went to her room to retrieve her goodies from the mall.

"I got a dress I'm just not sure about. I'm going to put it on and you tell me what you think."

While Lacey went to change Jane checked her cell phone. She had set it on silent for her date. There were 3 new voice messages and a text. The text was from Lacey, it was a picture of Lacey in the dress she was about to see. The most recent voicemail was from Wyatt and said 'Jane do not be immature, to not return my message is very unbecoming'. Jane felt her blood boil, delete. He had the nerve to tell people she was his girlfriend and she was the immature one. The next message was again from Wyatt that said 'Jane don't be silly about this afternoon. Please give me a call.'

The nerve, in two back to back messages he had called her silly and immature. Delete. Then there was a message from her mother. It said 'I want to hear all about your coffee with Wyatt. Call me, Love Mom'. That was odd she thought, had she even told her mother that she was going to meet Wyatt? Her phone chirped in her hands to notify her of a new text. It was from her father and said "Jane please call your Mother back to safe guard the sanity of an old man."

Lacey strutted back into the living room in a short black dress

"How do I look?" She hammed striking a pose. The dress was too short for Jane's taste but looked amazing on Lacey.

"Beautiful, it's a keeper. Hey I missed 2 calls from dun dun DUN, Wyatt. He had the audacity to tell me not to be immature. Grrr. Plus I have to call my mom and tell her how it went but I have no clue how she even found out about it in the first place."

Sensing her distress Ronald came and began head butting her shin until she reached down and scratched his ears. Content he came and sat next to her and allowed her to continue petting him.

"Do you think she is in cahoots with Wyatt?" Lacey wondered aloud.

"That would not surprise me one bit" Jane signed "I fully believe if she wasn't happily married to my dad she would try to marry Wyatt."

Lacey gave her a funny look.

"I don't think they'd actually ever get together in real life I just think that she thinks he is perfect and perfect for me, what I think doesn't really matter on the subject." Jane continued.

"You should take Gabe over to meet your parents; they'd be all like Wyatt Shmyrot." Lacey hooted.

"No way, I do not want him to find out my mother is certifiable. I should really call her back" Jane hemmed.

It was only 9:45, it wasn't too late. She willed inner strength and called. The phone call was painful. When asked what took her so long Jane replied honestly that she had a date. When her mother learned that date was not with Wyatt Jane sighed and rested her head in her hand. Jane finally even point blank told her she was not going to get back together with Wyatt. By the end of the called Jane looked exhausted.

"Chocolate?" Lacey asked already getting her out a piece. Jane pouted and nodded holding out her hand. Once finished she groaned

"Why does she have to drive me so crazy?"

"That's what mom's are for, sugar. They just want what they think is best for us." Jane rolled her eyes and Lacey continued "Come on think about it. How old was your mom when she married your dad?" She didn't wait for Jane to reply

"Wasn't she still in college? She's just trying to get you married so you can start making grandbabies." Lacey was clearly pleased with her assessment of the situation and with a flourish sat back down on the sofa and crossed her arms over her chest.

"Thanks for being my shrink; I'm going to call it a night."

Chapter Twenty-Five

She slept fitfully and moaned when her alarm sounded. Annoyed by the noise Ronald hissed at her clock until she turned it off. "Chill out Ronald, you get to sleep all day" she grumbled patting his head. She sleep walked through her shower, getting dressed and breakfast, put some coffee in a travel mug and headed to work. Most days Jane felt very capable and productive, today luckily her boss was at an offsite meeting, so she did the bare minimum and counted the minutes till lunch. At lunch she treated herself to a mani pedi. She was so tired she almost fell asleep in the chair as her feet soaked in the warm water and then were massaged.

Her real highlight of the day came when she received a text from Gage reiterating what a good time he had had and how he was looking forward to their next date. She quickly replied in agreement. Now with more energy she knocked out some busy work in the afternoon, simple filing that made her look much more productive than she had actually been. She took a long hot bath when she got home. Then munched on a bagel and cream and some baby carrots for dinner and then went to bed early with a book.

Lacey was temping in a call center this week and would be working a late shift. It was so quiet in the apartment Jane was asleep as soon as her head touched her pillow. Tuesday passed the same as Monday and it was Wednesday in no time. About an hour before lunch Jane got called up to the front desk for a delivery. As she approached the lobby, she saw a huge floral arrangement at the front desk.

She was thrilled until she saw who was delivering them, Wyatt.

"Beautiful flowers for a beautiful girl" he purred.

The receptionist was drooling.

"Wyatt what are you doing here?" Jane said flatly.

Her lack of thrall flustered him "We just left things so strangely..."

"Wyatt I am at work, thank you for the flowers but I have to get back. Bye"

Jane hoisted the flowers up and lugged them around the corner with Wyatt calling after her. When she got back to her desk, she was shaking. How dare he ambush her at work? And speaking of work, clearly her mother had struck again. She picked up her desk phone and called Lacey who was up and on her way the work. She told her about the flowers and her theory that her mother was in on it. Lacey was in agreement something was definitely up but unfortunately could not talk any longer because she had arrived at work.

She hung up and sat staring at the flowers on her desk fuming. She came very close to throwing them away but they were pretty. She went ahead and moved them to the lunch table in the break room. It took all of her will power not to call her mother and tell her to butt out of her personal affairs but she did not want to say anything she would regret.

Luckily with all of her fuming the rest of the day flew by. She took a quick jog around her block to de stress and clear her head for her date with Gabe. There was nothing like her run mix on her iPod and a pretty day to cheer her up. Must be the endorphins or something she thought.

She put her iPod in its dock in her room so she could keep jamming out while getting ready. She paused grooving out for a hot shower. She had previously decided what she would wear that night. It was a warm fall day, she went with a delicate short sleeved navy wrap dress, beige cardigan and a pair of brown peep toed kitten heels.

She wore a simple silver filigree pendant and silver hoops. She went a bit more dramatic with her eye makeup and did a semi smoky eye. She used brown shades so it wasn't too crazy. She brushed her teeth applied lip gloss and had just spritzed on some perfume when she heard a knock at the door. He was early! She did a quick spin in the mirror, turned off her iPod and headed to the door.

She checked Gabe out through the peephole. He was pretty dressed up, rocked a tie and jacket. She retrieved her clutch and keys from the table by the door and opened the door to greet him.

"Hey Jane, wow. I mean just wow! You look wow" he sputtered.

She gave him a hug and with her face on his neck inhaled. He smelled really good.

Pulling back she frowned and said "I feel a little under-dressed now."

"No way" Gabe interrupted "You look perfect."

Jane laughed "Well in that case..."

She closed and locked the door and they were on their way. In the car she asked how the school year was going. Gabe explained they were mainly doing a review of the previous year's work. It helped set a foundation of what areas they would need to focus on.

He inquired as to the world of finance. Jane explained how right now her boss was mainly working on returns for clients who had filed for an extension so their tax deadline was now in October. She went on to say

"Luckily when things are busy at work the day flies by." He had his mp3 player plugged into the car data port and offered it to her to pick out driving music.

As she browsed his library she was jazzed to see they liked a lot of the same music. Not that there weren't any bands that she had never heard of because there were. She went around a selected one of her all time favorite songs and turned to gauge Gabe's reaction.

He started drumming the stirring wheel and said "Awesome choice!"

It was just the reaction she was hoping for. He caught her eye and winked. They pulled up to an old school Italian restaurant with red and white checked tablecloths and candles on every table. They were seated and placed their drink orders then perused the menu. Jane went with a Chicken Parmesan while Gabe opted for home style lasagna with cheesy bread. The smell of the other patron's meals made Jane's mouth water.

"This is such a cute place" Jane murmured as they waited for their meals. "Have you been here before?"

"I love this place" Gabe returned "I believe it's the best Italian in town."

When their food arrived it was well worth the wait.

Jane actually caught herself moaning and looked up embarrassed.

Gabe teased "I know right, I'm amazed you have never been here. Aren't you from around here? It may be blasphemy that you have never been here. Just wait until you try the breadsticks."

Gabe went on to tell her his theory that these breadsticks alone could end all no carb diets out there. Jane wondered out loud how their pizza was and if they would deliver.

Gabe grinned "Have I created a monster?"

The portions were so large they each asked for their leftovers to be boxed up and Gabe ordered some tiramisu to go. They held hands as they made their way back to Gabe's car. Back at her place Jane invited him up so they could split the tiramisu. It was amazing, and Gabe let her in on another fact about the place. In the summer they made gelato. He even offered to take her. That really hit home for her, he was talking about taking her somewhere 8 months from now.

"I'd like that" she said "and thank you so much for tonight, it was wonderful."

She leaned in to kiss him on his cheek but changed her mind and went for it and kissed his lips instead. He responded wrapping his arms around her and deepening the kiss. Jane was just losing herself in the moment when she heard the front door open. They broke their kiss but kept their arms around each other.

"Well hello" Lacey said entering the living room.

"Hey, Lace" Jane said from over Gabe's shoulder.

Gabe turned his head and taking one arm from Jane's waist gave her a wave.

Gabe nestled his face into Jane's neck and murmured "I should probably be taking off."

She didn't want him to go but agreed that since they both did have to work the next day it was for the best. She walked him to the door and they shared another long kiss. Kissing Gabe was like getting a caramel frappuccino and licking off the bit of whip cream and caramel that peeks out from the top of the domed lid. She could kiss him all night, but grudgingly said goodnight and he was gone. She walked back into the living room to get a bottle of water. Lacey was sitting on the sofa with a bag of chips.

"Looked like it was getting pretty hot in here" Lacey said nonchalantly.

Jane looked upward and shrugged her shoulders. She sat down with her drink and when Lacey wasn't looking brought her fingers to her lips. They felt tender and in serious need of chap stick. It was a surreal feeling to have been in such an intense moment to now be watching Lacey eat chips. Lacey was a messy chip eater, she was getting crumbs all over herself. Jane shook her head, how could she even be thinking about Lacey eating chips and not Gabe after a kiss like that?

"Hey are you listening?" Lacey said raising her voice.

"Huh?" Jane answered.

"I'm sorry, my head was somewhere else."

"I'll bet" Lacey grinned "Well anyway I was just saying that Jack from Saturday night texted me."

"Who's Jack?" Jane asked looking confused.

"He's the guy I played the golf game with and then smooched the rest of the night. We are meeting up this weekend."

He was going to take her to one of those Japanese restaurants where they cook the food right at the table. Jane was fading fast and after displaying enough excitement over Lacey's upcoming date called it a night. She struggled to fall asleep even though she was so tired. She couldn't help thinking about Gabe. They hadn't spoken about when they would see each other again. She couldn't help but wonder if that was just an oversight or if maybe Gabe was not as into her as she thought. But, he had said the thing about the gelato.

She startled as her alarm sounded the next morning. Man, she did not want to go to work today. Jane turned her alarm off before it woke Ronald. Slowly she got up and ready for the day. She daydreamed and as she drove to woke, pulling into her usual parking spot she felt amazed that she somehow made it to work. Only eight more hours to go, she thought. Jane caught herself dozing multiple times. She went ahead and ate her lunch at her desk in an effort to catch up. During her break her phone chirped with a text from Gabe. "Thinking of you" swoon. She was instantly very awake, but unsure of how to reply.

Jane was always uncomfortable over text. She thought of maybe a dozen different things to say but could not decide so settled on a smile face. He replied back asking if she had any plans Saturday. She happily replied that she did not and they arranged a date for Saturday afternoon. Taking advantage of her new found energy Jane focused on her work with abandon and only ended up having to stay an hour late to get everything caught up.

She picked up some Chinese food on the way home. Once home she camped out on the sofa with her pjs on and caught up on her DVR queue. Before getting ready for bed she checked her email. Ugh, Wyatt strikes again. He had invited her to lunch with his mother and went on to say his mother could not wait to catch up with the both of them.

Huh? Jane scrolled back to the top of the email and realized he had not only invited her but her mother as well. There was no way she would be able to get out of this. She closed her laptop, popped an Advil pm and went to bed. When her alarm clock went off the next morning she actually felt well rested and ready to take on her Friday.

She went into the kitchen to make some coffee and saw a note from Lacey saying to stay up for her tonight. She added a "Will do!" and heart to Lacey's note and left it in the kitchen for her. She got to work and thankfully since she was able to accomplish so much the day before it was a pretty laid back day. She went ahead and bit the bullet calling her mother to see if she had seen the email from Wyatt. Not only had her mother seen it but, she had taken it upon herself to accept the invitation for the both of them. Telling Jane wasn't it so lovely that 'dear' Wyatt would set this all up.

Jane quietly sat at her desk and listened to her mother go on and on until when she finally could not take it anymore said "Oh darn, got to get back to work mom. Love you." Jane had never been confrontational so her biggest hope was that after this lunch Wyatt would just go away without her having to actually do anything about it. It was a pretty day out so Jane got a salad from a local shop and ate it in a park by her work.

Jane sat there soaking up the sunlight and fresh air. She wished she had brought a book to linger over and made a mental note to try to eat lunch outside until the weather became too cold to allow it. She grudgedly returned to her office. It was a co-workers birthday, so she happily snagged a piece cake.

On the way home she stopped by a bookstore. She perused the shelves for a good novel. She had been thinking of needing a good book every since her lunch break. She purchased a new release of one of her favorite authors. Her plan was to go home throw on some sweats and read her new book. She stretched out on the sofa and Ronald curled up on her hip. After moving around too often for his liking he slowly stretched and then padded to the far end of the sofa to curl back up.

She was buried in her book when she heard Lacey come in.

"Hey stranger" Lacey called out kicking off her shoes at the door. "I am so happy that gig is over, those hours were awful. Plus I think I already have something new lined up for next week. I got an email on my phone but couldn't open the attachment. I'll pull it up on the laptop after I eat."

Lacey walked into the kitchen and popped a TV dinner in the microwave, eating an apple as she waited for it to cook.

"So what's new, excited for tomorrow?" Lacey asked.

"Sure, but now I'm also dreading Sunday" Jane returned.

Lacey looking concerned asked "Why?"

Jane went on to tell her about how Wyatt had set up a luncheon with their mothers, and how without even asking her, her mother had accepted.

"Jane you have got to nip this in the bud. Just reply to all and say that you do not want to go" Lacey was in earnest. It drove her nuts to see her friend bend over backward to please everyone but herself.

"It's just lunch Lace" Jane began "and who knows maybe someday Wyatt and I could be friends again" That was a long stretch and she knew it.

"Friends?" Lacey asked dumbstruck "After how he left things when you broke up? After the stunt he pulled with Matt at the coffee place?"

The microwave beeped to indicate her dinner was ready

"You are so lucky, I am starving because I could have kept going" she said getting up to get her food.

Jane did her best to change the subject by asking if Lacey had talked to Jack since they last spoke. Feeling feisty Ronald began to swat at Lacey's fork while she tried to eat.

"Lay off Ronald" she said picking him up and putting him on the floor.

Lacey had known her long enough to recognize the subject change and between bites said "All I am saying is don't let them walk all over you and fine I won't say anything else and yes Jack and I have been texting quite a bit."

"I am not a good texter" Jane returned "but I do kinda wish Gabe would text or call more though."

"He's a teacher" Lacey replied "there are probably rules against that and plus isn't he fixing up his house or something." Jane had not considered that. It seemed very reasonable and cheered her up right away. Lacey went on to tell her more about Jack.

Given her usual aptitude for picking losers he seemed to have a lot going for him. He was a paralegal for a local firm and was also in grad school with the hopes of taking his bar exam becoming a lawyer. He did not go out a lot and was only at the bar the night he met Lacey because he was treating his little brother to a drink for his birthday. Lacey went on the say it was the little brother (Ian) who had encouraged Jack to hit on Lacey in the first place.

After they were all caught up Lacey asked Jane to watch a movie with her. About halfway through Jane was sleep. She awoke to a popcorn kernel bouncing off her forehead with Lacey trying to look as innocent as possible. She rallied and made it the rest of the movie then went to bed and crashed. The next morning she was thrilled to see

Gabe had texted her sometime last night to firm up plans for today.

He wanted to know since the weather was supposed to be nice, Saturday, if she would like to go on a picnic…at his house. She replied sure and laughed to herself that that probably meant the kitchen was still a work in progress. Given the time though she would have plenty of time to knock out a couple loads of laundry before she went. She started two loads and leaded back to her apartment. Normally she liked to guard her laundry but it was still pretty early she had a theory that anyone who stole other peoples laundry from a machine probably also slept in. She then toasted and bagel and opted for a cup a tea instead of her usual coffee and flipped through a fashion magazine.

Lacey walked in yawning and stretching.

"I love having a job lined up for a whole week but man those hours sucked. Hey guess what. I opened up that attachment I mentioned last night after you went to bed and it sounds like a good gig. It is a receptionist for an orthodontist with no end date AND the potential to go perm."

Jane congratulated her and added "That could mean a pay raise and health benefits right?"

Lacey attempted, unsuccessfully to nod her head and gulp some OJ at the same time. Lacey poured herself a bowl of cereal and Jane told her about Gabe's text.

"Oh rock on" Lacey replied "now you'll get to see his house. Try and sneak some pictures so I can see how grownups live"

With that Jane ran down to switch her laundry from the washers to dryers. When she got back, she hopped into the shower then modeled different looks for Lacey. She ended up going with a cute sweater dress, leggings and boots. Lacey needed no assistance picking out what she was going to wear. She showed Jane a slinky slow cut plum dress and some killer heels.

Jane shook her head at her and Lacey innocently shrugged what and said "If you got it is what I always say…"

Laughing her off Jane went to retrieve her laundry. She put it away before heading to Gabe's.

Chapter Twenty-Six

His place was only 20 min from theirs. She was there in no time. It was a cute neighborhood. The homes were older but appeared well maintained. Plus it seemed like almost every house took really good care of their yards. Many with little garden flags and mums planted for fall. Gabe's house was a 2 story brick colonial with black shutters.

Gabe met her at the door with his bulldog.

"Jane, this is Baby, Baby this is Jane" He said pulling her into a big hug.

"You have a very nice place" Jane said.

"Want a tour?" Jane nodded and they were off.

The first floor of Gabe's house seemed in decent shape. The foyer opened up into a living room with a comfy looking sectional sofa, ottoman combo and TV setup. She could tell Gabe had worked on the drywall in some places, but all the room really needed was a coat of paint. Next came what Gabe explained was truly the dining room but seeing as he didn't see any dinner parties in his near future, he had it set up as his home office. There was a desk and shelves up against one wall and a card table and chairs against another.

"Poker" Gabe said as if that was self explanatory.

It too needed a coat of paint and also was missing a light fixture. The dining room opened into the kitchen which was clearly a work in progress. There was new tile floor and there were base cabinets, but they did not appear to be secured to the walls. There was a nice stainless steel refrigerator, and a microwave on a cart in the corner.

"I'm waiting on my buddy, who is a plumber, to help me put in the sink and dishwasher lines" Gabe shrugged scratching the back of his neck.

Next was a small powder room. It was pink, very very pink. Pink wall paper, pink toilet, pink sink, pink tiled floor.

Jane giggled.

"I know, right?" Gabe said "I have clearly not started this room. Part of me wants to leave it this way, half of my friends refuse use it."

The stairs leading to the second floor sported some pretty retro gold shag carpet.

"Haven't even started up there yet, it's just mainly changing out carpet and pulling wallpaper" Gabe explained.

The last room on the main level was technically an office or den but Gabe had it set up as his bedroom. There was a queen sized bed with a blue comforter and a matching bed side table and dresser.

"Until I can get started on the second floor I just pretend I own a ranch, wanna see the upstairs? Be warned it's bad, very bad."

"Sure" Jane said curious.

"Just don't judge me"

All of the rooms, including the bathrooms shared the same gold shag carpet from the stair way. There were three bedrooms a hall full bathroom, and a bathroom off the master. The bathrooms shared the same retro color schemes as the pink bathroom downstairs. One hall bath was power blue and the master harvest gold. All of the rooms had popcorn ceilings and cringe worthy wallpaper. The worst was in the master. It was a shiny metallic floral print.

"Wow" Jane said taking it all in.

Gabe went on to explain how when he had first purchased the home the first floor looked a lot like the second floor before he worked on it. It was bad wallpaper and popcorn ceilings everywhere.

"Hungry?" Gabe asked as they headed back downstairs.

Jane followed Gabe through the kitchen and out a door to a backyard brick patio. Baby charged ahead of them and happily romped around the fenced in backyard. There was a blanket and a basket laid out next to the patio.

"How cute" Jane cried.

Gabe sat down and began unloading sandwiches, sides, plates and glasses. Jane sat across from him with her legs curled to her side.

"Soda, iced tea, or lemonade?" Gabe asked.

Jane went with lemonade and a turkey sandwich.

"You make a great sandwich too!" Jane complimented.

"It's all in the bread selection."

Baby investigated a tree a squirrel had recently ascended as they ate their sandwiches and shared some chips, macaroni salad, and watermelon.

"We are lucky it is so nice outside today" Gabe remarked stretching out after finishing his plate.

"The weather has been so crazy recently" Jane returned "It was pretty cold and gross out earlier this week."

"Either way the whole picnic thing would not have happened otherwise" Gabe returned "Would you like to watch a movie?"

They cruised by a video kiosk and agreed on a super hero movie. Once back at Gabe's he popped the movie in and went to make some popcorn while the previews were playing. Even though he had a sectional capable of sitting at least 6 he handed Jane the bowl of popcorn and sat down right next to her.

Jane found it hard to concentrate on the movie once Gabe put his arm around her. She could feel body heat radiating from his thigh to hers and from his arm to the back of her neck. She leaned into him and relished the butterflies in her belly. Trying to be as discreet as possible she snuck peeks at him doing her best to keep face forward but using her peripheral vision.

He had clearly shaved this morning and was missing the stubble she remembered from the sports bars. He had a way of laughing during the funny parts that she liked. He would smile just enough to make crinkles in the corners of his eyes and sort of chuckle exhaling out of his nose. Very, very cute she thought. And his killer blue eyes, she could just stare into them all....oh wait. She was so caught looking out him.

Even though the movie was still on she couldn't hear a word. Everything got very still as one corner of Gabe's mouth curled up just before he brought his lips to hers. To say the kiss was intense would be putting it lightly. She put her arms around his neck and he pulled her into his lap. He held her tightly as he moved his lips from hers to her neck. At this Baby jumped on the ottoman and began barking excitedly at them.

Jane giggled and Gabe buried his face in her neck.

"You suck dog" he mumbled as Jane scooted off his lap and straightened her dress blushing.

He rubbed his hand over his face and said "come on Baby, time to go outside." He was back in no time and sliding in next to her said "Where were we?"

Any hope for concentrating on the movie was over.

"Your hair smells so good" Gabe said nuzzling his nose behind her ear "like coconut."

She was supper ticklish there and Gabe grinned at her having found a weakness. He kissed her again. He tasted like a sweet tea and popcorn which was a surprisingly yummy combo. His hands were on her back and she felt herself pressing into him. Her mind was racing between tearing off all of his clothes and not wanting to seem over eager but to be honest all of this kissing and body contact was really turning her on.

He had to be feeling the same way she thought. She wondered if he would make the next move. A loud rattling noise came from the back door.

"Sorry" Gabe said coming up for air "that's Baby wanting to come back inside. If I don't get her soon she is liable to break the screen door....again"

He detangled himself from her and headed towards the kitchen. Jane took advantage of the breather to use the very pink bathroom. Luckily her makeup hadn't rubbed all off. She applied some chap stick and headed back to the living room.

Gabe was turning the movie off and when she entered the room and said "So I'm thinking we should turn this lunch date into a dinner date. That is if you can stand my company much longer?"

"I'd like that" Jane replied

"Well the kitchen is not up for cooking yet so we can go out or maybe...order in"

There was some definite inflection on the word in.

"I think we should order in" Jane said felling bold and locking eyes with him.

He didn't break eye contact with her as he slowly walked over to her. He took her hands in his and leaned her against the wall. When he kissed her she felt her toes curl.

"You are so beautiful" he whispered into her ear then playfully nipped it.

She seriously felt like her knees might buckle. She let go of his hands and wrapped her arms around his neck. His body molded to hers.

"Whew" he said taking a step back "you should come with a warning label."

He turned and holding her hand sat her down at one end of the sofa and jokingly sat himself at the other.

"Jane I am really into you" he began "and I really don't want to mess this up. Part of me wants to blow all caution to the wind but I don't want to rush you. What are you feeling?"

Jane moved to sit next to him and taking his hand in hers said "I really like you."

She nestled into him and they sat there for a few moments feeling the weight of their words both spoken and unspoken.

"Alright" Gabe said "let's talk more about ourselves. Likes and dislikes." They ordered some Chinese delivery and talked for hours. Favorite books, movies, and colors you name it. They both liked comedies; Jane preferred the romantic ones to the gross humor ones. Gabe also loved action movies; Jane liked those too but mainly the super hero ones versus really suspenseful ones.

Blue was both of their favorite color. Jane's favorite season was spring and Gabe's summer because of the break. They talked about their families and any travelling they had done.

Gabe still had living Grandparents on his mother's side; they lived not far from where Gabe's parents wintered in Florida. Jane had all four of her grandparents still living. Her dad's parents lived in Ohio and my mother's parents lived in Virginia. He was still very close with his grandparents, travelling down to see them most summers. This one he had not because he was working on his house.

Jane wasn't as close to her Grandparent's. She saw her maternal grandparents more often than her paternal simply due to distance. He spoke more about his brother and sister in law and their kids. It was clear to see how important family was to him. Jane told him about her dad and how out of everyone she never felt pressure from him, not like she got from her mother.

Gabe was pretty athletic, he enjoyed most summer sports. Loved being in the water, whether it was jet skis, kayaking, surfing, boating. He loved the ocean, or any lake he was not particular. He was not crazy about winter sports preferring to be inside where it was warm. Jane was not as athletic, she liked to go for walks and go to the beach but she had never done anything other than swim.

She loved to read while he sheepishly admitted he had not read for pleasure in a really long time. They went on to describe what their perfect day or evening would look like. Gabe's would be a barbeque at the beach with a group of his favorite people. Jane's dream day would have her handling her favorite pieces of art. Her eyes sparkled as she talked about being able to run her fingers over their brush strokes. Bummer was even if she was able to handle these pieces she would never in a million years touch one for fear of damaging it.

Gabe laughed out loud at that imagining the look on

her face if she was ever in the position. It was so late that it was now morning. They had talked almost all night. Jane just didn't want to leave. They stretched out side by side on Gabe's comfy sectional. Gabe playfully kissed her chin and feeling a second wind she kissed him back more forcefully. Gabe pulled his head back to look at her in question. She nodded pulling him towards her. Realizing the direction they were headed, Gabe led her to his room.

Closing the door behind them he said "Are you sure?"

She was never more sure of anything and laying down on his bed reached her hand out to him. He placed his hand in hers and she pulled him onto her. Covering her, kissing her with his hands in her hair Gabe only pulled back when he realized Jane was trying to pull his shirt off. Sitting up he pulled it off and threw it somewhere. Jane kicked off her boots and socks off laughing.

Searching her eyes for approval Gabe lifted the hem of her dress. She raised her arms over her head as he slid it off of her. Her hands moved to her waist to take off her leggings. Gabe stopped her, easing her back down onto his pillows. He started kissing the skin exposed from the top of her bra and then moved kissing her stomach as he slowly dragged the material down her legs and continued kissing her skin as it became visible.

She felt like she was going to explode she wanted him so bad. She sat up reaching around him to tug on his belt in an effort to loosen it. Gabe groaned and slid off of the bed. He kicked he shoes off and removed his pants and socks. He left his boxer briefs on and lay back on the bed facing her and pulling her into him arms. Jane could not stop touching him, pulling him against and kissing him.

Gabe explored each inch of her as it was uncovered. He was so thoughtful and gentle stopping to ask her if everything felt alright multiple times. His body was beautiful she thought running her hands over his chest and back. He was only the second person she had ever been with.

Afterward laying in his arms, his lips on her forehead he said "I am in so much trouble with you."

At that she pushed into him and they started all over again.

Chapter Twenty-Seven

Walking up in his arms was one of the most peaceful moments Jane could ever remember. He started stirring and tightened his grip around her

"Morning beautiful" he said with one eye open giving her a kiss on the neck. "So what are we going to do today and please say it will not include clothes?" She giggled and then sat up quickly pulling the sheets with her.

"What time is it?" Jane suddenly asked panicked.

"Um like 11ish" Gabe said checking his watch.

"I am so sorry, I have to meet my mom for lunch" she said throwing her clothes on. "I can't be late."

"That's cool" Gabe said pulling on some pants "Do you want me to make you some coffee?"

"I am so sorry for running out of here, like this I just have to get home and showered" Jane said leaning over and giving him a quick kiss and then grabbing her purse headed for the door.

"Can you tell me when I'm going to see you again before I get a complex?" Gabe joked.

They agreed on seeing a movie they had both talked about earlier the next night. Jane would call him after her lunch to firm up the details. She waved through her window as she pulled away. She daydreamed about her night with Gabe the whole ride home. She had never experienced anything that good during her entire relationship with Wyatt.

Why couldn't she just email everyone and tell them the truth? That she didn't want to go and that she didn't even want to be friends with Wyatt. As much as she wanted to she did not want to disappoint her mother. Still she would have to figure out some way for Wyatt to focus his attention elsewhere. She flew into the apartment and slammed the door behind her with a bang.

"Lacey!" she called out as she ran into the bathroom.

"Coming home in the clothes you left in yesterday, I knew you had it in you" Lacey laughed as she walked into the bathroom.

Jane had already jumped into the shower so Lacey peppered her with questions as she sat in the sink counter. Turning the shower off and grabbing a towel Jane went to her room with Lacey trailing behind her.

"I have no idea what to wear" she moaned.

Lacey picked out some tailored gray slacks and a green twinset. Jane not up for arguing, got dressed while Lacey poured her a cup of coffee. Jane let her hair air dry and threw on the bare minimum of makeup she could get away with and ran out the door. Lacey shook her head as Jane headed to the restaurant. She got there only a moment behind everyone else. It was a beautiful place in the heart of downtown. It had a huge picture window that overlooked the sidewalk. They were seated right in front of it.

Wyatt's mother sat on one side of Jane and Wyatt on

the other. When they sat down Mrs. Huntington took Jane's hand in her own and told her how devastated she was when the two of them had broke up. Jane almost laughed out loud, yeah right she thought. Wyatt's mom now her biggest fan, how things have changed.

They ordered their food. As they waited Jane watched people walking up and down the street. Once their food arrived she ate quickly. Maybe too quickly, she thought as she had nothing to keep her busy while she watched them eat. She excused herself and went to the ladies room.

She would have stayed in there but it probably would have upset her mother. When she got back to the table she was relieved to see the dishes had been cleared. Then dismayed to learn they had ordered desserts. Wyatt boasted that he had ordered the lite sorbet for her.

Great she thought now wishing for a trough of chocolate pudding instead. When their desserts came she did her best to enjoy the sorbet. It was a bit chilly for a frozen dessert she thought. Wyatt seemed to have dropped something because he was now kneeling next to her. She lifted the tablecloth and peered under it.

Until he took her hand in his and pulled at a small velvet jewelry box. She felt as though she was watching a slow motion horror movie. She both felt his hand on her hand but also felt as though her hand was not even attached to her body. She didn't even feel as though she could even hear what he was saying. What she heard was air rushing.

Why couldn't she speak? Why couldn't she shake her head no? She watched in horror as he slipped the ring on to her ring finger. Movement on the other side of the picture window caught her attention. She looked up to see Gabe staring open mouthed at her. She brought her hand up to cover her mouth.

Her left hand. Which was now sporting a giant rock on her ring finger. He shook his head and walked away only to look back at her a few steps away then continue on his way. Why was he there? This is not happening; this is not happening she kept repeating in her head.

"Jane, darling say something" her mother said coming over to her.

"Ahhh" was all she could muster. She frantically looked back to where Gabe just was and then back to her mother. She stood and Wyatt enveloped her in a tight embrace. All around her the other patrons were smiling and clapping for them. With what everyone in the restaurant assumed were tears of joy streaming down her face.

"Jane really?" Wyatt admonished handing her a napkin to dry her eyes "don't make a spectacle."

She pursed her lips and nodded. On demand she held her hand out to both her mother and Wyatt's mother. When lunch was finished Wyatt walked her to her car letting her know the engagement announcement would run in next Sunday's paper. Also, that they would need to set aside time to arrange her things be moved to the home he just purchased. He said he would swing by her place tonight and grinning patted her on the backside.

She moved away from him and got into her car. What the hell had just happened she screamed internally. She called Lacey but could not coherently speak to her so Lacey gave up and told her to just tell her when she got home. Also, to pay attention to the road and not get into an accident on her way home.

She pulled over a few blocks away and tried to call Gabe. It went straight to voicemail. She looked at the ring on her finger, how in the world would she ever get out of this. It was strange she thought how this very moment was everything she would have wanted 3 years ago. How things have changed.

What she wanted was so obviously different but her not being able to stand up for herself was clearly the same. She held her head in her hands. Taking a deep breath she sent Gabe a text. She asked that he call her so she could explain. Figuring that was all she could do she drove home.

Chapter Twenty-Eight

H er phone had rang multiple times on her drive back. Each time she reached for it she hoped it was Gabe. Each time it was not the calls were actually from either Wyatt or her mother. She ignored them all. Once home she burst through the door.

"Lace" she cried out.

"In here!" Lacey called back from the living room. Lacey looked up as she entered the room "How was lu…." She began but was silenced when Jane held up her hand with the ring on it. "Um, I'm lost" Lacey continued "how did that happen?"

Jane told her everything including seeing Gabe

"And you just sat there?" Lacey said still looking at the ring.

Jane nodded glumly "What do I do?"

Lacey put her hands up and said "Um tell Wyatt you do not want to marry him but say you lost the ring on the way home and give it to me"

Jane huffed "I'm being serious Lace."

"So am I. Here let me try that baby on" Lacey returned holding out her hand.

Jane rolled her eyes and handed her the ring. Lacey cradled her hand and murmured sweet nothings to the it.

"Jane, do you want me to marry him?" she joked.

Lacey stopped joking after Jane told her about the forthcoming engagement announcement and the expectation that she would be moving in with him.

"No I have to do this, I have to return the ring and tell him that I do not want to marry him" Jane said "but how do I tell him that?" she continued.

"Um like you just did. Hi Wyatt here is your ring back I do not want to marry you" Lacey replied.

Jane shook her head that just seemed too harsh. Besides she had never ever stood up to Wyatt how was she going to be able to do it now. There was a knock at their door. Jane cringed and Lacey motioned for her to stay where she way as she got up to check who it was. It was Jane's mother.

"I know you are home Jane" she called out through the door "I parked next to your car."

Lacey opened the door "Hi Mrs. Martin."

"Lacey" she said walking past her and into the living room. "Jane you left so quickly, before I was able to tell you how happy I am. You were so quiet at the restaurant."

"I know mom, I'm so sorry" Jane began.

"Let me see the ring" her mother asked reaching for her hand.

"I have it" Lacey called out rushing over.

"Why in the world are you wearing Jane's ring?" she gasped.

"I ah, well um" she said taking it off and handing it to her. "I'm going to go get a drink" she said slowly backing out of the room as Mrs. Martin frowned at her.

"Here darling" she said handing the ring to Jane "Let me see it on your hand."

Jane held her hands in her lap. Her mother reached over and pulled her left hand towards her and slide the ring on it.

"Really Jane you are acting so strange. You should be so proud of yourself you have landed quite a catch"

"I've got to get out of here" Jane said getting up. Leaving her mother open mouthed on the sofa, she set the ring on the coffee table, grabbed her keys and ran out the door. She checked her phone before she pulled out, still no response from Gabe. Figuring it could not hurt to try she made her way to his house. When she got there she was happy to see his car parked in the driveway.

She got out of the car and went to knock on his door. No answer. She knocked again, still no answer. Her head drooped and she turned to walk back to her car. Halfway to her car she saw Gabe a few yards away walking Baby. She straightened and waved. He nodded but didn't seem thrilled to see her.

"Where's your fiancé?" He said in greeting.

"I'm not engaged Gabe, look no ring" Jane said holding up her hand.

"That was not what it looked like earlier" Gabe returned "So that was the famous ex boyfriend?"

Jane nodded chewing her lip.

Gabe sat down on his porch steps and ran his fingers through his hair. "I really like you Jane but I do not know how to handle this. I mean after last night." he said looking up at her.

Jane lifted her hands and shrugged. "I don't know what to tell you. I do not want to marry Wyatt or even date him."

Gabe regarded Jane and then asked "Does he know

that, and, who were those other people with you?" Gabe asked.

Jane looked down "Our mothers" she then looked up to see his reaction.

He exhaled deeply laughed. "Jane this guy just proposed to you in front of your mother's, how can you tell me you are not together?"

"My mother thinks we should be together and I am not sure why his mother likes me all of a sudden. But that doesn't matter because I don't feel the same way."

Gabe stood and moved for the door "I just need some time to process all of this, okay?"

"Of course" Jane said stepping back "I didn't mean to intrude."

Gabe sighed and pulling her into his arms said "Come on don't be like that. This is just a lot to deal with"

Jane, with her face in his neck inhaled trying her best not to cry. When she felt Gabe's arms open she took a step back and giving him an awkward wave got into her car and left. That was so embarrassing she thought driving away. Of course he would have no interest in dealing with this.

She returned to her apartment and was relieved to see her mother's car was gone.

"Do not ever do that to me again" Lacey called out from the living room as she walked in the door.

She grimaced as she entered the living room.

"Your mom lost it when you took off. I have never seen her that pissed" Lacey continued. "So where'd you go?"

"To Gabe's" Jane mumbled

"How'd it go?" Lacey asked.

Jane scrunched her nose and shook her head. She went to put her feet up on the coffee table when something caught her eye, the ring. She picked it up. It was actually very pretty, very big and very pretty.

"Why did he propose?" she moaned.

Lacey snorted.

"How are you laughing right now?" Jane asked annoyed.

"Come on, I mean come on…you are turning down Wyatt Huntington's marriage proposal. I am just thinking of how different you were two years ago" Lacey said grinning "Please tell me you see a little bit of irony in all of this" she went on.

Lacey had a point Jane had to admit. It had been a long time since Jane had any interest in Wyatt. She couldn't not even point to the moment she stopped loving him. It had happened slowly over time.

"What did my mom say when she left?"

"Something about disowning you" Lacey winked. "She just does not get why you aren't thrilled. She even mentioned something about taking you to have your head examined."

At this Jane picked up the closest thing she could find. It was a throw pillow and tossed it at Lacey.

Catching it she laughed "It's your mom, you know exactly what she said. That and she wants you to call her once your home. Probably should have told you that when you walked in the door.

Jane went to grab her phone. She had a bunch of missed calls and texts from Wyatt. She had every intention of continuing to ignore those. She called home. Thankfully her dad answered. She spoke to him for a bit and he let her know without a doubt he supported her one hundred percent in whatever decision she made. He did however want her to know that in his personal opinion she did not seem very happy when she dated Wyatt.

She heard her mother in the background telling him that was crazy. He gave her his love and passed the phone to her mother. Her mother went on and on about all of Wyatt's qualities and that he had called her and told her that Jane was not answering his calls. She sat there patiently saying um hum from time to time. After 5 minutes of this she was holding her head in her hands.

She apologized and promised that she would call Wyatt back then hung up. She knew she wasn't going to call Wyatt. She sat on the sofa and worried at her nails. Then it hit her Wyatt said he was going to stop by tonight. She had to get out of there. She apologized to Lacey and told her that she was going to go spend the night at a hotel.

Lacey stared at her open mouthed "Jane you know I love you but that is the craziest thing I ever heard. Your problems will not go away just because you do" she said.

"I just can't deal with this tonight" Jane murmured.

"Fine, but don't run away. Here give me your phone" Lacey replied reaching her hand out.

Jane cautiously handed her phone to her. Turning it on Lacey promptly replied to one of Wyatt's text. She wrote 'Hi Wyatt it is Lacey. Jane must have had something that didn't agree with her at lunch and is going to bed sick. She will text you or call you tomorrow' and sent the message. Jane let out a sigh of relief and took her phone back from Lacey, thanking her.

Chapter Twenty-Nine

Lacey paced back and forth across the living room. "This whole situation sucks babe but I think Gabe is a good guy and if you give him a day or two maybe he'll be able to think about it and be okay with it. The important thing is that you have already told him how you really feel so it is up to him at this point. Do I know for sure if he can get past this? No, I don't. All I know is it is not something you can control so to a certain extent you have to let it go so you don't drive yourself crazy worrying about it."

Lacey was right Jane knew. She sat down abruptly and folded her arms over her lap. There was nothing else she could do when it came to Gabe at this point but she didn't want to just sit there and wait to hear from him either.

"Let's go get a drink" she said standing.

"Music to my ears" Lacey smiled.

They went to a local pub. It was a hole in the wall located in a strip mall. The place was a total dive but sometimes you just needed to go somewhere you would not care how you looked. It was mainly empty which was good.

Lacey and Jane sat at a table in the corner and Lacey went to go get them a couple of beers.

"Do you really think I'll ever hear from Gabe again?" Jane wondered aloud.

"Babe, you got to let it go because it is out of your control" Lacey countered.

Jane rolled her eyes and took a deep swig of her draft. She was not a huge fan of beer; she normally preferred the sweet tasting drinks, but this place had really good happy hour deals though so dollar drafts are hard to pass up. Jane slapped her forehead realizing her issues had completely taken over the whole weekend. So much so that she had not even asked Lacey how her date with Jack had gone. When she asked, Lacey blushed which was out of the normal for her. Jane had a pretty good feeling that Lacey enjoyed herself quite a bit.

She told Jane all about her night. She even had another date scheduled with Jack. Jane thought it was really cool Lacey was seeing someone with a set schedule. In the past she seemed to gravitate towards the artsy type and that was really code for the unemployed. Lacey glowed talking about their evening and hopefully would not get bored with him as she tended to do. For their next date they were going on a river boat.

"How romantic" Jane gushed.

"As long as I don't get motion sickness" Lacey worried.

"You'll be fine" Jane assured her.

They had finished their drinks so Jane went up to the bar to get their next round. While she waited Lacey put some money in the pool table so they could play while they drank. Lacey may have been master of arcade games, but Jane was really good at pool. Jane silently wondered to herself if Lacey was doing it just to try and cheer her up. It was nice given the current situation to just focus on something other than Gabe or Wyatt. After a couple of games the girls walked back to their apartment.

The following week flew by like a blur. Jane tried multiple times to speak to Wyatt about the proposal but every time she either chickened out or he was unavailable. Finally Friday night while Lacey was on her riverboat date he agreed to stop by for a chat. What she intended to be a serious talk Wyatt had assumed would be a booty call. She spent the evening pushing his hand off of her thigh.

Finally at her wits end she declared "Wyatt I do not want to marry you."

That stopped him cold. He stood and brushing the wrinkles from his slacks said "You might pretend that you think that, but you and I both know that I am all you ever wanted. I'm doing you a favor here, don't forget it."

He lowered his mouth to hers and gave her a crushing kiss pushing her forcefully against the back of the sofa then left. She tenderly lifted her fingertips to her lips and gingerly felt them. They felt a bit puffy but no worse for the wear. What had just happened? She thought. He had completely ignored what she had said. Was it going to take her not showing up on their wedding day for him to take the hint. She picked up her phone and called her mother.

Finding willpower she did not know she had possessed she point blank told her that she would not be marrying Wyatt. She may have even thrown in a come hell or high water even though she was not completely certain it applied. After a long pause she could hear her mother crying on the other end. Shit, she thought maybe she should have eased her mother into this.

"Mom, don't cry. I'm so sorry I yelled., Mom please say something" Jane worried into the phone.

"I just don't want you to die an old maid" her mother sobbed back. Jane had to stifle a giggle, was that all? She went on the have a heart to heart with her mother that they probably should have had years ago. Her mother still saw her as a young girl who needed her help and come on Wyatt honestly did look really good on paper. Besides since Jane hardly spoke to her mother how would she know she had moved on? In her mom's mind Jane was still pining over Wyatt because that was the last Jane had ever told her.

When Jane went on to assure her that she not only no longer loved Wyatt but had also met someone new her mother was thrilled. She wanted to hear all about Gabe which Jane was happy to share until she had to tell her he had witnessed the proposal. Her mother was horrified for her and now completely understand her behavior in reacting to what should have been should a dream come true.

"Oh Jane what are you going to do?" she asked sympathetically. She told her how Wyatt had stopped by and she had tried to end the engagement. Her mother was furious on her behalf and suggested that she and Wyatt come over for dinner. There was no way she concluded that he could continue this arrangement if she stood up to him with their help.

That was a brilliant idea Jane agreed. They spoke a few moments longer and then Jane thanked her mother and told her how much she loved her. When she hung up she sat motionless for a few moments. There are times when her mother would just blow her mind. She had been so certain that her mother was going to be an obstacle that she would have to overcome in all of this.

As she sat there she felt like crying at the realization that all her mother wanted for her was for her to be happy. She felt pretty silly being so nervous to tell her the truth. Ronald padded over and jumped into her lap. At his affection she did begin to cry. She knew she always would have

Lacey having her back it was just really liberating to know she wasn't the only one.

It was a happy cry. She sent Wyatt a text asking over to dinner at her parent's the next night. With any luck this would all be a distant annoyance by Sunday she hoped optimistically. Her emotional conversation with her mother took a lot out of her. She crashed early with Ronald curled at her feet. When she woke he was in a ball maybe an inch from her nose. Each breath she took would make his fur move slightly.

She tried getting up with disturbing him but he was a light sleeper and mewled in protest at her movement. Picking him up she went downstairs and fed him. She wasn't very hungry so she drank some orange juice and surfed the web until Lacey came downstairs. Lacey looked pretty guilty and came over to warn Jane that Jack had spent the night.

"Hoochie mama" Jane replied and turned back to the computer.

"Just be cool when he comes downstairs" Lacey pleaded.

Jane crossed her eyes and made a fish face "So I can't talk to him like this?" she asked.

"Jane!" Lacey stressed.

"Alright, alright. I'm cool" Jane promised "So how was it?" she asked saucily.

Glancing upstairs Lacey began fanning herself and said she would dish when he left. Lacey went back upstairs and a few moments later both she, and Jane could only assume, Jack came downstairs together. Lacey went into the kitchen to make coffee while Jack sat awkwardly on the sofa.

Jane waved and said "Hello."

"Hi Jane, it ah nice to see you again" he replied.

"Did you want to watch TV?" Jane asked motioning towards the remote.

"Is that okay?" Jack asked.

"Sure" Lacey replied walking back into the room with two steaming cups of coffee.

She sat down close to him handing him a cup. He rested back with his other arm across the back of the sofa giving her shoulder a squeeze.

Jane had to stop herself from saying 'awww'. She had to admit they looked very cute together. Jack was taller than Lacey but then again who wasn't? He had dirty blonde shaggy hair, just long enough to pass the tops of his earlobes. He set his coffee down and turned on the morning news.

"Would you like anything for breakfast?" Lacey asked "I can make eggs, or bagels?"

He said he was fine but encouraged her to get something if she was hungry. Lacey said she was fine to and leaned into him to watch the news. Jane smiled to herself. There was no way Lacey would eat by herself in front of a guy she liked. Lacey invited Jane to come over and sit with them. She turned the computer off and came across to sit in the armchair by the sofa. Jane asked Lacey what their plans for the day were. Lacey pouted saying Jack would probably have to leave soon because he had a big test coming up next week.

He laughed and kissing her the side of her head said he would much rather be hanging out with her. With that Lacey seemed appeased. When they finished their coffee, Jack got up to put their mugs in the kitchen and then went upstairs to collect his things. His test was Wednesday night so as he left he confirmed dinner with Lace for Thursday. She agreed then after a long kiss he was gone.

As soon as the door shut Lacey ran to the kitchen to toast and bagel.

"I am so hungry" she mumbled munching on a slice of cheese as her bagel toasted. Jane followed her and once her bagel popped put another one into the toaster for herself.

"I take it last night went well" she said as Lacey consumed one half in no time.

"He is so friggin hot Jane. You never expect it with the preppy types. I swear I'm amazed I didn't throw my back out last night" Lacey gushed.

She poured herself another cup of coffee and took her time with the second slice. "After dinner when he brought me back here we were kissing in his car for a little bit and then he started kissing my neck. I almost jumped him in the car but managed to talk him into coming inside" Lacey went on. She seemed so happy, Jane was thrilled for her. Before Lacey would tell Jane all of the gory details, and she made Jane told her about Wyatt's visit.

Lacey wasn't surprised. Of course God's gift to women would never believe someone would not be into him. What did shock her was Jane's mother's reaction.

"Go Mrs. Martin" she hooted.

"I know, right?" Jane replied.

"Can I please please please please come to dinner too?" Lacey pleaded "I have got to see this."

Jane while welcoming the additional support really thought it would be best if she did this on her own since they both could admit Lacey would have a hard time keeping her mouth shut. Jane promised to give her the play by play and soon as she got home and Lacey relented agreeing it was probably for the best. Later on the girls ran to the grocery store to stock up.

Once home Jane got ready for dinner while Lacey napped. She really hadn't gotten enough sleep the night before. She wore some navy slacks and a white sweater with some brown boots. As she stepped out she turned right back around to grab a trench and an umbrella to avoid getting soaked given her white sweater. She got to her parents before Wyatt and gave her mother a long hug.

Her father then came to pat her on the back "Never been prouder of you Janey, can't wait to watch you dump this jerk."

"Dad!" she cried.

He just raised his hands like 'what?' and winked at her.

She took the ring out of her purse. Her mother had found an old ring box for her to put it in to return to Wyatt. When he arrived he acted like the night before had never happened. He pulled Jane towards him and kissed her on the cheek.

"Hello Mom, Dad" he called out cheerfully.

Her father sneezed what suspiciously sounded like the word asshole and went to go sit in the living room. Wyatt rested his arm around Jane's shoulders as they followed him. When she went to pull away he pulled her tighter to him smiling at her. Her father was sitting smack dab in the middle of the sofa and her mother was sitting on the loveseat. She could have kissed them. Seeing there was nowhere for them to seat together Wyatt sat in one of the Wingback chairs while Jane went and sat next to her father. After he sat Wyatt attempted to engage her father in some small talk.

"Not now young man, Jane has something she would like to tell you" her father interrupted.

Jane motioned to the box on the coffee table and after taking a deep breath said "Wyatt I asked you here tonight to, in front of my parents, let you know that I do not love you and cannot marry you."

Wyatt sat there quietly while Jane and her parents

214

wondered what to say or do next. When he rose suddenly Jane's father did as well.

"Wyatt, Jane does not want to hurt your feelings and would like this to be as amicable as possible."

"Amicable?" Wyatt spat. "Our announcement is running in the paper tomorrow."

"Maybe you should have asked Jane if she even wanted to date you before you went ahead and proposed to her." Jane's father replied.

Wyatt looked down at Jane and said "I don't believe you."

"How can you not believe me?" Jane asked rising.

"Trust me you will come to your senses, this can be very profitable for all of us" Wyatt went on

"Profitable?" Jane asked while her father roared "You listen here young man."

Jane put her hand on his shoulder and he slowly sat glaring at Wyatt.

"You poll well" Wyatt replied. "If I am going to run for office, I need a simple wife, no one too showy. You fit the bill and it will be like winning the lottery for your family. Seriously Jane, think of how much you can improve your lives" he went on.

Having heard enough Mrs. Martin at that point interjected "Wyatt why on earth do you think marrying you would equal winning a prize? I'll have you know we are quite content in our situation and do not need nor desire your saving us. I believe I have heard enough, young man. Kindly take that all rock no style ring and get you uppity ass out of my home and off my property."

She said all of this while sweetly sitting.

Wyatt picked up the box and walked out of the room calling out "You'll regret this" as he left.

Jane looked at her mom and started clapping while her dad went over and gave her a big kiss.

"I like it when she gets feisty" he said winking at her

"Oh Mitch hush" she said blushing "now let's go eat dinner. I made Beef Wellington and now we don't have to worry about that idiot ruining our appetites."

Dinner was delicious and Jane had so much fun hanging out with her parents. She thanked them both after giving them big hugs and kisses then went home leftovers in tow. As promised when she got home she gave Lacey the play by play.

"Shut up" Lacey exclaimed eating some leftovers "he compared himself to winning the lottery."

Lacey was beside herself and was so bummed that she had missed it all. What she would have given to see the look on his face as Jane's mom kicked him out. Jane admitted it was something she would not forget. At the end of it all she just felt lighter and happier then she had all week. Sure she had no clue what would happen with her and Gabe but she was able to acknowledge that either way she would be okay.

Chapter Thirty

The next day she made a special trip to the store just to buy the paper to see the announcement. Lacey tagged along and they read it right there in the middle of the store. It wasn't just any old announcement it was a half page gigantic announcement.

"Oh my god" Jane said staring at it.

A good chunk of the announcement was taken up with a blown up picture of them from college. Once she read the announcement she cringed. There was no way Gabe would ever trust her after this. She folded the paper up not wanting to read the whole thing in the store. Lacey ran to go buy them some donuts and they returned to their apartment. Donut in hand she read it out loud once there.

"Mr. and Mrs. Wyatt Huntington II happily announce the engagement of their son Wyatt Huntington III to Miss. Jane Theresa Martin. Wyatt and Jane met and first dated at Virginia Commonwealth University. Wyatt went on to Graduate school in Chicago while Jane entered the workforce after graduating. It was followed by comments like 'Jane will of course no longer be working as she will stay home to raise their family ' and 'We are so thrilled welcome Jane into our family'. The newspaper even had a supposed quote from Jane saying 'We can't wait to start our own family after the wedding.' The paper went on that given the prominence of the groom's family the wedding which was slated for the following spring would likely be the event of the season with all of the who's who to be invited.

Jane sunk down in the armchair uneaten donut still in hand. "It say's I want children Lace" she said dumbstruck.

"Holy shit" was all Lacey could manage.

"How do I undo this?" Jane asked. "Everyone in town will think we're still engaged and with that fake quote from me they are going to think if anything that Wyatt ended it because come on he is a friggin winning lottery ticket."

"Holy shit" Lacey repeated.

Jane set the donut down and putting her head between her knees did her very best to not hyperventilate. Lacey came over and gently patted her on the back. Her phone starting ringing at that point.

Lacey checked it and said "It's your mom."

At that Jane grabbed the phone and answered it "Mom have you seen it?" there was a pause as her mother responded "I know it is horrible. I never said that, is that legal?" another pause then placing her hand over the mic she said to Lacey "My mom says my daddy is going to kill him" she then uncovered the phone and said "tell dad not if I get to him first."

They spoke a bit longer and then hung up.

"What am I going to do?" Jane grumbled "How can I get everyone to know that we are not engaged and that I broke it off?"

"I'm not sure babe, but I know we will think of something" Lacey said sympathetically.

Jane's phone rang off the hook that day with calls to

congratulate her. When she checked in with her parents she learned it was pretty much the same for them. She finally gave up and turned her ringer off. That evening flipping through channels with nothing on Jane stopped on college basketball since the Rams were playing. It was bitter sweet because it reminded her of her bet with Gabe over the game they watched together at the Sport's bar.

"Whatcha watching?" Lacey asked walking in.

"Basketball" Jane said pouting.

"Hey the athletic director reached out to the choral department to see if they would sing the fight song at the next home game" Lacey said.

Jane went to bed early since she was dreading work and people talking about the announcement.

The next day her desk was crowded with all the females who worked on her floor. They were asking when the date was and if they could see her ring. She said there was no date and it was a long story about the ring. She smiled politely and tried to discourage any additional discussion on the matter. When her boss came in he asked her pointedly if she would be resigning anytime soon. She tried to explain the situation as briefly as she could to him but did her very best to assure him that she was not engaged and would not be resigning any time soon.

He seemed very sympathetic to her assuming that Wyatt had dumped her. She tried to let him know that it was more of a misunderstanding that he had proposed and she had declined but not in enough time to stop the announcement. What struck her was he clearly did not believe her. It was almost as though he pitied her, like she was concocting this story. It was embarrassing, this was someone who knew her and knew her family. Was this how it was going to feel every time?

Her mother drove out to meet her for lunch. She was

trying to cheer her up. She kept the conversation light as she watched Jane push her food around on her plate. She finished lunch and her mother drove her back to work. When they pulled in she was surprised to see several media vans crowded around her office building. Her mother looked at her in question and she shrugged. Her mother went to drop her off in the front of the building when the news people began rushing the car microphones out asking Jane for a comment.

Her mother put the car into reverse as Jane called her boss to ask what was going on. He told her the news crews had arrived just after she left for lunch and that it was okay for her to lay low while they figured out what was going on. Next she called her father to see if there was anyone at their house. He had no idea what she was talking about but at her direction looked out the window and informed her confusedly that the coast was clear. Her mother quickly drove them to her home as Jane scoured news pages on her cell phone in an attempt to learn what this was all about. When they arrived she switched to searching for info on her parent's computer.

"What on earth is going on?" her father asked confused by all the drama.

Jane gasped when she discovered what prompted all of this. She brought one hand to cover her mouth looking at her parents her other hand pointing to the screen. Her parents both leaned into to read and her father who didn't have his glasses asked her mother to read it out loud.

"It is an official press release from Mr. and Mrs. Wyatt Huntington II saying that they regretfully confirm the engagement of their son to a Miss. Jane Martin is dissolved due to previously unknown flaws to her character. And, they ask that their son's privacy be respected at this difficult time."

At that her mother made the sign of the cross and her father started cursing.

Tears running down her face Jane turned to her mother and said "How can they do this?"

Her mother pulled Jane to her and rubbed her back murmuring that she didn't know. Her father had left the room to call his attorney to see if this could be subject to liable. Her mother led Jane to the sofa and offered her tissues. Her father on the cordless came in and poured all of them a shot of brandy. Jane accepted readily and threw it back raising her glass to her father for another which he granted and then left the room when his lawyer came on the line.

Jane and her mother waited for him to hang up. He came back into the room frowning. When Jane asked what happened her father came and sat on the other side of her and putting a hand on her shoulder said his lawyer believed the press release and insinuation of a flaw was vague enough that there was no legal action available to dispute it. That a flaw could imply something as simple as bad credit score to lord knows what. Jane buried her head into his shoulder.

They sat like that for some time and listened to the home phone ring off the hook. The machine picked up and Jane leapt to grab the phone when she heard Lacey's voice. Lacey was panting and between breaths asked why their apartment was covered with reporters looking for her. Jane apologized for not thinking to tell Lacey the news. When she explained the situation she had to jerk the phone away from her ear as Lace lost it. They spoke for a while and Jane finally ended the call letting Lace know that she was spending the night at her parent's house, admitting that she was so emotionally exhausted that she was ready to pass out. The two shots her father had given her may have helped.

She called out sick from work the next day, figuring her office may be staked out by news crews again. It must have been a very slow news week if a broken engagement garnered this much attention. Part of her just wanted to bury her head in the sand and avoid the whole situation. When she brought this up as a possible solution to her mother it was made clear to her that one way or another there would be a response to this falsehood. She would not allow Jane's reputation be tarnished in this way.

Jane could not really understand how it would affect her in the long run, but knew it pissed her off in the short term. She thought about various options even considered trying to stage her own rebuttal press conference but by the time her father's lawyer reached out to one of the news stations it was considered old news and they weren't interested in her side anymore. Only the week before reporters had stalked her and her family trying to get a comment, and now no one was interested. The current news dominating the community was how well her university basketball team was doing.

There were expectations that they would qualify for the upcoming playoffs. Wyatt had won she thought. Even though this time around she was the one who had broken things off he had spun it to the world out of spite. That bothered her more than anything, well that and how upset her mother was. She thought about taking out a full page ad in The Dispatch but it seemed so desperate that she was nervous it would not feel believable.

At least it was safe to go to work and back to her apartment. Ronald had missed her, but Lacey had taken good care of him. She sat with him on her lap and stewed. Lacey being dramatic paced from one side of the room to another coming up with one wild plan after another. She suggested buying a billboard, a plane with a message trailing behind it. Print fliers and post them on all the electric poles in town.

"Now that is just environmentally cruel" Jane joked.

She was flipping channels on the TV and stopped when she saw a basketball game and that the Rams were playing. It was almost the end of the game and it was a close one.

Then Lacey started jumping up and down going "I've got it, oh man, I've got it. If this would work. Oh it's such a good idea" excitedly.

"Huh" Jane replied confused.

"Okay so the choral director reached out to the drama director who I'm still tight with to see if any of the actors from the musical wanted to participate and I might help out."

"Okay, I'm lost" Jane said.

"So the Rams have been crazy good this year and the next game is a big rivalry game so it is going to get a ton of coverage" Lacey said as if that made sense.

"I still don't get it" Jane repeated.

"So I might be able to put you in the halftime show" Lacey went on "Just think about the local undivided attention of all of Richmond."

"Um that sounds like my worst nightmare" Jane said shaking her head.

"It might be you only window of opportunity to set the record straight in your our words" Lacey said pointedly.

"We don't even know if people thinking I'm flawed is the end of the world, who doesn't have flaws?"Jane argued.

"Seriously, the way your phone has been going off?" Lacey asked "Besides don't you want to tell people you never said you wanted to start a family?"

"I don't want to embarrass him" Jane said.

"Are you kidding? After what he just did to you?" Lacey asked.

"Lacey, you and I both know even if I wanted to do it there is no way I would be able to speak in front of that many people."

"I think you are braver than you know" Lacey replied solemnly.

Lacey who wasn't much of a sports fan even sat down to watch. They won in the end and the local news came on right after. The broadcast began with film from local bars and restaurants where fans had gathered to cheer on the Rams.

"This is pretty cool how well they are doing" Jane said.

"Just think about it, okay." Lacey said before she went to bed.

As Jane lay in her bed she replayed the recent events in her mind. So much of Jane's life she had spent like a pretty doll in an unopened box. She had been taught that it is the unopened toy that has the higher resale value. She had always done what her parents asked and never even considered rebelling. She went to the right school. She even dated the right guy, even though he was so wrong for her.

That was it, she thought to herself deciding Lacey's idea might be her only chance to publicly stand up for herself. Maybe there is no happy ending in life. Maybe the guy who you really like will not get past the fact that the entire city you live in thinks you're not worthy to be engaged to someone else. No matter what happened with from this point on Jane had to take a stand now or she may never. That was how Jane had found herself, mic in hand, center court halftime of the Rams George Mason game.

Chapter Thirty-One

A t Jane's direction Lacey had pulled some strings with the athletic director of VCU. She booked the VCU choral dramatic troop to sing the school song during half-time while the drill team performed. What they did not know was Jane would be making a public service announcement first. Once all the players were off the court and Lacey had the performers set up, Jane walked out on to the court.

Winking at her, Lacey handed her the mic. The crowd assumed that Jane would be introducing the performers. Instead after taking a deep breath and cringing at her image on the score board she began

"Good evening Richmond. My name is Jane Martin. My recent engagement, and now more recently, end of my engagement to Wyatt Huntington the third has been widely reported. The stated reason for this is a flaw in my character. I have come here today to tell you all that this is true. I have flaws. This specific flaw in my character is that I never stand up for myself. I'm trying to work on that, starting with me being here today. Wyatt was my first real boyfriend and I liked him so much that I lost sight of who I was before we met. And then on the day we graduated from this university, when I thought he was going to propose to me, he dumped me instead. It has been over two years since that break up, and I have learned so much during that time about who I am and what makes me happy. When Wyatt recently moved back, he wrongly assumed that we would just pick things up where we left them. But that was impossible because I wasn't the same girl he dated back then. I want to be very clear and honest about what my character flaw was. I made a mistake in not just flat out telling him that I didn't love or want to marry him until it was too late to stop the newspaper announce-ment, and for that I am truly sorry for any embarrassment I may have caused him or his family. Thank you for hearing me out, Go Rams!"

Jane handed the mic back to Lacey and calmly walked off the court with the Rams fight song echoing all around her.

Lacey ran after her and pulled her into a big hug. "You were amazing!"

By that time local reporters were making their way over to them shouting out questions to Jane.

"Um, let's get you out of here" Lacey said grabbing her hand and pulling her to the nearest exit.

They made a clean getaway. Lacey pulled over into a parking lot to catch her breath.

"Did I really just do that?" Jane asked Lacey with a sideways glance.

"You sure as hell did, there should be no question now. Holy crap Wyatt has got to be losing his mind right now. I do think went too easy on him though." Lacey giggled.

"Hush" Jane said pushing her shoulder.

"He deserves worse for everything he has done over the

years" Lacey went on but then seeing the look Jane gave said "Alright, alright I'm done."

When they got back to their apartment, Jane was shocked to see Gabe waiting by her door.

"Hey" she said uncertainly "what's going on Gabe?"

He held up his phone with a video of her at the game. "Matt is at the Rams game and sent me a video he took of the halftime show. He thought I would really enjoy it. I'm also pretty sure it may have already gone viral on Youtube too, just so you know."

Jane covered her face with her hands.

"Pretty public way for clearing up the status of your engagement" he laughed.

"I suppose. Hey Lace, can we have a sec?" was all Jane could manage in response.

"Sure. Good seeing you Gabe" Lacey said before heading inside.

"So the thing is I would still like to keep seeing you if you would like to still see me" Gabe said looking pretty nervous.

"I do want to keep seeing you" Jane began "but, I want to take a bit a time first to let all of mess that may come from what I did today settle down first. Maybe lay low for a bit"

"I'm good at laying low" Gabe said grinning.

"Not that kind of laying" Jane laughed flushing.

"You don't have to deal with this all alone though" Gabe replied more seriously taking her hand.

"That means so much to me Gabe, but I don't really know how to explain this so bear with me. I feel like I need to take a bit of time to center myself. I feel a bit adrift and can't really meet you in the middle feeling this shaky about myself."

"I deserve that" he said hanging his head. "I never

should have let the whole situation with you and your ex bother me as much as it did."

"Gabe" Jane said stopping him "Don't be crazy, if the roles were reversed I would have done the same thing. Believe me I really want to pick up where we left off of, if I think about it any longer I may just drag you upstairs right now, but"

"But" Gabe repeated.

"But" Jane continued leaning against him "I just want the dust to settle first."

"Just please don't leave me hanging too long." he said kissing her forehead.

He left looking back at her with sad eyes.

She went inside and relayed their conversation to Lacey.

"Did I do the right thing Lace?"

Lacey stared at her open mouthed "I thought you really liked Gabe."

"I just feel like I need a break" Jane confessed suddenly looking very exhausted. "I think I'm just going to go lay down" she gave Lacey a half smile and went to her room.

Jane was out as soon as her head hit the pillow. Ronald came and snuggled into her neck. Luckily her phone was downstairs. Lacey fielded calls from local reporters and sent a call from Wyatt straight to voicemail.

When Jane woke the next morning she felt so refreshed. She had had a vivid dream of this beautiful bridge. The idea of it symbolizing everything that she was going through really struck her. It was the concept of moving from one situation to another, point a to point b. Before Wyatt had come back into her life she had actually thought she was over him.

While she had no romantic feelings for him in any capacity at this point, she at least now could admit that he still had some power over her. If he had not she would have had no issue telling him from the start to seek greener pastures elsewhere.

Sure she had spoken up for herself yesterday, if front of what felt like the world. She cringed remembering what Gabe had said about it being on Youtube. Even though she had faced a giant fear yesterday, she felt that his power over her would not truly be gone until she could look him in the eyes, and truly stand up for herself.

What the bridge in her dream reminded her was despite all her bravery yesterday she had not crossed that bridge yet and would not be able to say those words to Wyatt until she had. She also felt that while Wyatt was an obstacle she would need to overcome possibly what she feared the most was disappointing her mother. She had never even told her parents about Gabe before her heart to heart with her mom. He was a perfectly nice guy but she still wondered if her mother would think he was good enough compared to Wyatt?

As Jane mulled that thought over Ronald began head bunting her knee in search of attention. She picked him up and carried him downstairs to feed me. Lacey had the news on and they were showing film footage of a fender bender on a local bridge. Setting Ronald down quickly Jane watched reminded of the bridge from her dream. It was not the same bridge on the news but it made her wonder if her bridge was real and maybe even local. She really didn't understand why but she really wanted to put that image onto canvas.

Offended by his abrupt descent and now obvious lack of breakfast, Ronald mewled loudly at her feet. Realizing this Jane apologized to her disgruntled feline and filled his bowl. When she came back into the room Lacey asked her why she was acting like a space cadet. Jane told her about her dream and the feeling that the bridge was familiar.

Lacey laughed saying "Um we live in The River City so there are plenty to choose from."

That was not a bad idea Jane thought "Want to come check some out with me today?"

"Bridges?" Lacey asked.

"Yep" Jane replied happily getting up to get some cereal.

"Will there be a lot of walking?" Lacey asked nervously.

"Probably not I was just thinking about driving around" Jane said in response.

With that, Lacey agreed to go.

"Bring your camera" Jane called out from the doorway and then waited for Lacey by her car.

As they drove Lacey caught Jane up on all of the calls she had missed. Jane had to laugh at her can response to all of the reports who called. "Jane Martin has no follow up remarks to her public statement yesterday. She would however like to remind you that prior to yesterday she did reach out to you and you were not interested in any of her comments at that time."

"If I ever need a press secretary the job is yours" Jane replied. She was dreading listening to Wyatt's message though.

They drove out past Jane's parent's house and down Patterson Avenue. There was a cemetery on the left and Jane was struck by the trees that lined the road in front of the cemetery. There were power lines running above the trees and each tree had been severely pruned to avoid the lines overhead. The deep cuts into the crown of each tree resembled a gaping mouth. That along with the cemetery behind them gave them an overall creepy look. Jane shivered to herself then asked Lacey to snap a picture of them and drove on.

They started with the World War II Veterans Memorial Bridge that was part of route 288. It felt like the longest bridge not that the James River was wider beneath it as it covered a stretch of farmland as well as the river. Jane had Lacey take a couple of pictures as they passed over it and then once crossed Jane turned west and then cut back towards the river to take a couple more pictures. It was not the bridge from her dream. While it was long it wasn't very inspiring.

Now on the south side of the river, they continued east down Robious and crossed the river again. This time they took the Willey Bridge with Lacey protesting that they should have stopped at Stoney Point to shop on the way. This bridge was definitely more interesting than the last. It curved and winded with river vegetation folding in on both sides. Again Lacey took a couple shots as they passed over. Finding a spot to take a long shot picture from was a bit tricky but not impossible.

"I thought you said we wouldn't be walking" Lacey groaned.

"Come on, it's like an adventure" Jane was having the best time.

Lacey was just mad that she had stepped in a puddle and now had squishy shoes. The bridge was more interesting than the first but it still wasn't the one from her dream. When they got back to the car, Lacey took her shoes off and set them in the back window to dry. They crossed to the south side again this time on the Huguenot Bridge. It was similar to the 288 bridge but not as high above the water. The water, below it, was like glass with less trees or rocks breaking the surface. Lacey didn't even need reminding to take pictures as they crossed this time but blaming wet shoes waited at the car as Jane went to take some pictures from the ground.

"I'm starving" Lacey said as they made their way to the Powhite Parkway Bridge.

Getting closer Jane said "Shit it's a toll road do you have any change?"

Lacey did and as they crossed Jane pointed south "What's that bridge? Take lots of pictures."

"I don't think that's a bridge for cars, maybe it's for trains" Lacey said studying it.

Once back on the north side they stopped for food. They ate in a hole in the wall sandwich shop and Lacey peppered Jane over the whole bridge thing. Jane could not explain it, but she felt like the concept of a bridge was speaking to her. Lacey rolled her eyes but this was the most excited she had seen Jane about anything so she just shrugged and went along with it.

They're next bridge was The Nickel Bridge. They looked up in advance whether it was toll or not to make sure they had enough money for it. It was, but they had change from lunch so they were covered.

As they approached the bridge Jane began slapping Lacey on the shoulder "This is it. Take pictures, take lots of pictures."

"Ouch, stop hitting me and I'll take pictures. Geez" Lacey shouted.

Once over they took the first exit, Jane parked and got out to take more pictures. Once she got back in the car Lacey asked

"Are we going home now that you found your bridge?" Jane wanted the cross one more which they would have to do anyways to get back home. It was a bridge they were both already familiar with being close to downtown. The Lee Bridge, from it Jane got a two in one because the

Manchester Bridge was close enough to the east for Lacey to also take pictures of as they crossed.

Lacey's shoes were dry enough that she agreed to walk around with Jane. What made this one special was that it had a pedestrian suspension bridge that ran beneath and crossed over to Belle Isle. During the Civil War the island had been used as a Prison for Union soldiers. Lacey always thought the place was creepy because so many people had died there.

Jane took more pictures, even aiming across the river towards Hollywood Cemetery. She was having a terrific time, until some kids on bikes asked if she was the chick from the Youtube video. She figured that was her sign to go home. On the way back she stopped by a pharmacy and printed all of the pictures they had taken.

Once home she laid them all out on her bed while Lacey took a nap. She set her easel up and starting with the bridge from her dream, using pastels to draw it. She would refer to the photos from time to time, but mainly just drew from memory. The pastels she used gave her piece a soft smudgy effect. She lost track of time and had to get up to turn on her overhead light because it had gotten so dark outside. Her drawing wasn't complete but it was close. She stretched her arms and walked downstairs.

Lacey was still awake, snacking on the sofa while she watched Real Housewives of somewhere. Jane made herself a bowl of ice cream and joined her. Ronald smelling her food started crawling all over her for a taste. She gave in and let him lick some off of her spoon. She told Lacey about her drawing, sending her upstairs to check it out.

Lacey came back down mouth dropped. "Jane that is beautiful."

Jane blushed and thanked her.

"I think I might try and do all of the bridges" she admitted.

She wasn't sure if she would be able to do it but she felt really inspired. She was actually bummed that she would have to go to work tomorrow. She would have preferred to stay home and work on her project. She must have been hunched over pretty bad while she drew though because her shoulders and back felt pretty sore. When she finished her ice cream, she left the bowl for Ronald to lick and went back upstairs to take a bath.

She ran the water as hot as she could stand it and added some shower gel to the mix to make it a bit bubbly. The bath was so hot she could just barely stand in it, feet burning, for a couple minutes before she dared to sit. Once she was all the way in, she relaxed and let the hot water uncoil her abused muscles. As she lay there she began to formulate a plan.

There were nine or so Richmond area bridges that crossed the James. If she could drew them all she would bring them to that Gallery downtown to see if they had any interest in showing them. She decided to hold off on contacting Gabe until she was done. She wanted to practice putting herself first for a change. The water was so wonderful she was in danger of falling asleep. Once she felt completely like mush, she got up and changed into comfy yoga pants and an old t-shirt.

She didn't feel like making anything for dinner so she had a bowl of cereal. She filled Lacey in on her plan to see if the Gallery might have any interest in her work. Somewhere, she still had the contact information of the guy at the gallery. She had to laugh at herself, here she had barely finished one piece and she was dreaming of an art show.

For Lacey her demeanor seemed remarkable, given all

of the recent stress. She wondered though how long Jane would put of listening to Wyatt's message.

Jane spent the evening doing random internet queries as to the possibility of showing her work. It all seemed very confusing and boiled down to who you knew at first. She was encouraged to see that since there was a healthy art community in Richmond, there were various venues that may be interested. What she was surprised to learn was that it may be simpler then she had originally assumed.

She figured out that once she had completed her project of all the bridges she would need to take a picture of each one, she would then save the files to a disk, then the disk could be submitted to local gallery's. Depending on their focus, they could elect to show her work but she would need to figure out what to price the pieces and the galley could get up to 50% of the profit.

It was late though and since she was dreading work the next day she turned off her computer and went to bed. Work was a trial. Luckily there weren't any reporters but that did not stop her co-workers from gawking at her most of the day. Her boss could tell how uncomfortable she was and told her she could leave early. Once back home, after finally finding that business card she called the gallery, asking for Adam. After explaining her plan he agreed to get the gallery owner to preview her work.

She felt giddy hanging up the phone. Taking a deep breath she sat down to listen to Wyatt's voicemail.

"Hi Jane, gotta say I didn't see that one coming. I really did love you and I hope everything works out for you. Goodbye"

She didn't delete the message knowing Lacey would want to hear it. Wyatt was actually not being a jerk about the whole. Wonders never cease she thought shaking her head and got right back to her drawing. She planned to approach each bridge at a different time of day. Her current piece felt mid day with a clear and bright sky. It was almost complete, she really only needed to sign and seal it. She took a step back from it taking it in. In its design the dark steel interlocking triangles were bold against the cloudless blue sky. The James River below it seemed quiet and calm. She had done the best she could to recreate the image from her dream. She wanted to it to feel as peaceful as it had to her.

She started stressing out again about work the next day. Finally giving up she called her boss at home to ask if they was any way she could take some vacation starting the next day. He did not seem thrilled by the short notice but Jane had been such a good worker and since her father was a good friend he agreed. It felt like a giant weight was lifted off of her now that she could devote this time to her bridge project.

She could not really explain it to her parents or her boss but she really felt like she had to do this. She could finally acknowledge that she never really moved on after her break up with Wyatt. Sure she had an apartment and a job, but she was not creating anything. She was living a place holder life and she would never be happy unless she did something to change that.

This felt right to Jane, like a way to speak for herself, without having to interrupt any future basketball games. She got started on the next bridge right away. Her perspective for the bridge across route 288 was a winter morning, the sun just a glow from behind the farms on Robious. The bridge was more simple in design versus the first one she had drawn. The real movement of this piece was the gradation of the colors in the sky. There was an orange glow emanating from the southern tree line to the charcoal gray of the retreating night sky. The river below the bridge boasting the white tipped wake of a now unseen boat.

Lacey's return from work roused Jane from her drawing. She ran downstairs to greet her and get some food. She had not eaten all day and munched on some chips as she made a sandwich. Lacey filled her in on her day. She was really enjoying her gig at the orthodontist's office. When she finished her food she brought Lacey upstairs to see what she was working on. The Nickel Bridge picture was complete and the Route 288 Bridge was fairly complete.

"Which one will you do next?" Lacey asked, sorting through their photos.

"Maybe the Willey" Jane send pointed to one in Lacey's hand. "I think it would look really cool with fog" Jane continued.

"Oh I totally am with you there" Lacey replied.

Walking back downstairs Lacey asked "What happens when you have finished them all?"

"I spoke to Adam from that gallery and he seemed pretty interested but it truly comes down to the owner" Jane replied.

"I was actually wondering about Gabe?" Lacey said.

"I'm still all about Gabe. I just want to finish this first. He can be very distracting."

"Jane!" Lacey exclaimed trying her best to seem shocked. "What about your job?" she continued.

"I'm not going to quit or anything. I've taken a bit of vacation to work on this" Jane replied.

The rest of the week she worked almost nonstop breaking for food and sleep and halfway through a shower at Lacey's request. She had completed 8 pieces and was working on her ninth. It was the Manchester Bridge, at nighttime. The reflection of the moon glowing from the river and the Wachovia Towers, not that Wachovia even existed anymore she just didn't know what people called them now. It didn't feel finished but she could not figure out what it was missing. At one point she considered adding a man looking over the edge in way contemplating his own mortality, but it felt too morbid.

Then she remembered that she had read once that an eagle nested somewhere high on one of the downtown office buildings. She finally added a large predator like bird perched on the side of the bridge looking into the river. Possibly for his next meal, it made it feel less ominous and more hopeful at least for the bird versus the fish.

Out of vacation time, she went back to work. That evening she had been invited to her parents for dinner. She brought her portfolio with her and set them up one by one, in the kitchen. She borrowed her mom's newish digital camera to take a picture of each. Then saved them to a disk, as requested by the gallery. Once the disk was finished she held it in front of her nose and squeezing her eyes tightly shut she whispered a wish to the disk that the people of the gallery like it.

She was like this when her father walked into the room. Blushing she wrote her name on it with a magic marker and then slipped it into an envelope. Her father winked at her and came over to her artwork and looked at each one by one. She had used different mediums, oil, watercolor, pastel, pen, and charcoal. They each had a different feel but the same theme, movement, change.

"Jane these are really good" he said proudly.

"Thanks dad" Jane said beaming "I'm going to submit them for consideration, at an art gallery downtown."

"That sounds very important, Janey. A proper artist. I am very proud of you, sweetheart. You have been through quite a bit these last few months and.." He was interrupted by the dinner call.

Her father gushed and gushed so much about her work that her mother gave up and left the table to go look at it right away. She rushed back into the room giddy, clapping her hands.

"Jane they are so beautiful" she said sitting back down.

After they ate, she brought out some cookies. Which made Jane laugh because every time her mother brought out cookies it made her feel like she was seven again so hopeful she would get more than one. She had three. She collected her things and returned home. Lacey had been out on a date with Jack. This may have been Lacey's longest relationship since college, Jane thought and was happy for her. She wondered if maybe Lacey had held herself back from committing in relationships to not hurt Jane. Sometimes Jane wondered what she had ever done to deserve such a good friend.

The next day on her lunch break, she rushed over to meet Adam and the owner Phil, at the gallery. When she walked in Phil stopped her asking if she was the girl from the basketball game video. Blushing she nodded, reaching out to shake his hand.

He elbowed Adam "Why didn't you tell me, she was the girl from the video?"

"What video?" Adam asked waving to Jane.

"You have got to see this" Phil said taking his phone out.

"hm hm" Jane murmured trying to catch their attention.

"Oh I'm sorry" Phil said putting his phone away "you brought us a disk of your pieces."

"Yes" she said taking it from her purse and handing it

to him. "How soon should I hear back from you?" she asked.

"Very soon" Adam said reassuringly.

She went back to work and had to stop checking her phone. She did her best to focus on her work, since she had to be realistic, there was no way she would hear back from them today. Once home, she took a long bath with bubbles. She purposely left her phone in her bedroom so she would not keep looking at it. Trying to de-stress and just let the universe do what it may was harder then she thought. Giving up she put on pajamas and went downstairs to watch TV with a bowl of ice cream. Ronald curled up in her lap, wanting to lick the spoon.

Lacey came home from work not long after. She had to work a bit late since they were working on a file organization to delete the patients who had not had an appointment in 5 years.

"Very healthy dinner" she remarked nodding at the bowl in Jane's hand.

"You are what you eat" she grinned.

"How'd the gallery thing go?" Lacey asked kicking off her shoes.

"The owner recognized me from the video, but I don't know if that's a bad thing. He seemed excited about it. I just need him to be as excited about my work."

Lacey joined her in having a bowl of ice cream herself for dinner as well. "How's Jack?" Jane asked.

"I really like him" Lacey said smiling.

"Maybe we can all go out some time so I can get to know him." Jane went on.

"That's a great idea, maybe dinner and a movie?" Lacey replied.

"I'm game" Jane agreed.

"Why don't you call Gabe and invite him?" Lacey asked.

Jane shook her head "I don't know what to say to him."

"How about I miss you, and want to see you again?" Lacey said sweetly.

"I still feel so embarrassed by the whole thing" Jane said "Maybe soon."

There was a comedy, they had both wanted to see and Lacey was pretty sure Jack did as well so they set it up, for the following Saturday.

Thursday morning, Jane heard from Adam. He let her know they were very interested in setting something up. They had been looking at the work of a local sculptor as well and thought their pieces would work together enough to have a show. He said that they would draw up a contract and if she was agreeable and the other artist as well they could set something up for as soon as three weeks from now. She gave him her email address for him to forward a contract to. She sat at her desk shaking her hands as she waited for it.

She forwarded it to her father, so he could confirm it was legit. Once she had his okay, the gallery set up a joint meeting with her and the sculptor. Her father went with her, for moral support but waited in the car. She was a bit early and was there before the sculptor. She sat and small talked with Adam until he arrived. She stood up surprised that it was Gabe's friend Matt.

"Hey Matt" she said warmly "I didn't know you were a sculptor."

"Are you the other artist?" Matt said giving her a hug.

"I am" she replied.

"Busy girl" he said winking.

The owner Phil brought his laptop over to them and pulled up each of their pieces one by one. Jane could tell why he thought they would work well together. Matt's work was abstract mechanical metal pieces that did seem to speak to the bridges she had drawn in an almost engineering way. Jane wondered what Matt thought of her work. She didn't have to wait long because placing his hands on the table, he said.

"I'm in, what do you say Jane?"

She smiled and said "Sign me up."

The owner seemed thrilled and asking them to rise and follow him explained to them how he intended to lay the pieces out. Jane's pieces still needed to be professionally framed but he knew a guy and it was part of their contract that he take care of that portion of the styling. He wanted them to have a thin silver frame and a thick white beveled mat. Jane agreed happy that was how she had pictured them as well. Matt had 12 pieces and he would stagger their pieces along the walls with 3 to a wall. One wall with two of Jane's pieces and one of Matt's and then the next with two of Matt's and one of Jane's and so on and so on.

The three largest pieces of Matt's would be on pedestals spaced out in the center of the room. Jane could see it all laid out in her mind. The gallery itself was on the small side but still in the hip section between Carytown and downtown. It had a restaurant on one side and a boutique on the other. With polished dark thin planked hard wood floor and in the entrance area exposed brick walls gave way to long white walls. It had high ceilings, that were a light gray. Phil hoped to advertise an opening in a couple local papers and on line. He also had a mailing list of client's he believed the pieces would speak to that he wanted to invite.

He asked that in the next day or so they prepare their own guest lists, as the first evening would be not open to the public. They would each be allowed to invite ten people due to fire code. One big step they each would need to take was deciding how much to sell their pieces for. Jane was nervous and asked if she had to sell all of them.

"How many do you want to keep?" Phil asked.

"Just one" Jane said thinking of the bridge from her dream.

"That fine" Phil said explaining that they would just list that one as not for sale. He asked Matt if there were any of his pieces that he did not want to sell as well.

"Nope" Matt said grinning "I'll be thrilled if they all sell."

As Jane's pieces were all the same size he suggested the oil piece be priced at $400 and the other pieces $350 to $300 with the more colorful priced higher. For Matt's pieces he wanted to price the largest ones at $500 and the smallest $200 depending on size, having them range. Jane did the math in her head. That was over a thousand dollars if her pieces sold. Once the meeting was over she spoke to Matt for a bit.

He worked for a local non-profit and sculpted in his free time. She asked him if he was going to invite Gabe as one of his ten people. He asked if she wanted him to.

"If it's alright, I would like to invite him" Jane said.

"Of course" Matt said "I think he would like that."

"Alright, well don't tell him you saw me today just let him get the invitation in the mail okay" she was earnest.

He promised and, after giving her a hug, left. She ran over to her car. Her father was waiting patiently.

"Who was that young man, Janey?"

Jane explained that not only was he the sculptor that she would be exhibiting with, but she actually already knew him. She told her father about Gabe and how they had left things. She also explained that she hoped he could come to the show as one of her guests and maybe it could be a fresh start for them. Her father thought it was a lovely idea and that Gabe sounded like a nice fellow.

Jane thought long and hard over what ten people, she would invite. She had five spots after her parents, Gabe, Lacey and Jack. She would like to invite her boss Mr. Hamilton and his wife Claire since he had been so good to her this whole time. There were two of her former art professors that she would also like to invite. Other than that, she would check with her mother to see if there was anyone else she should ask. She called her mom on the way home and after talking to her decided her last invite should go to one of her mother's girlfriends.

Once home she emailed her former art teachers and explained what she was doing. They seemed thrilled, in their responses and gave her their home addresses for the invitations. She emailed the information to Phil then took a deep breath. This was actually happening, she felt amazed. The show would be two weeks from this Friday. She enlisted Lacey to help her get a great outfit.

They spent that Saturday at the mall going from store to store. Lacey laughed at how stressed out Jane was getting over what she would wear. Jane admitted to not feeling stylish enough to be having a show and being very nervous about what people would think of her. She gravitated towards black dresses but then felt like she was only doing that because that's what she thought an artist should look like. She felt like a fraud.

Lacey took over at that point banishing her to a dressing room and bringing her dresses to try on. Nothing felt right. It was winter, she wondered why was every other dress was sleeveless. She was so over the having to wear a cardigan all the time. She let Lacey know, that while she did not know what she wanted to wear, she knew she wanted sleeves, short or long.

Lacey returned from her next search and brought Jane six or so dresses. When Jane picked up the Kelly green one, she knew it was it without even trying it on. It was a jersey material wrap style dress. The sleeves were somewhere between short and three quartered length and the skirt hit the top of her knee. She bought some charcoal grey hose and had a pair of black heels that would look amazing with it.

When they got home, Lacey's invitation was in their mail. After she opened it, and read, it she handed it to Jane. It was so beautiful she thought. There was a picture of one of her pieces and one of Matt's. She ran her fingers over the raised lettering of her name. This was unreal.

She thought it odd that she did not hear anything from Gabe. He should have gotten his invitation, then it hit her. Since both she and Matt were showing, he would assume it was Matt that invited him and not her. What could she do to let him know that she wanted him there? She could not think of anything, so she just let it go, figuring no matter what hopefully she would see him there and then she could talk to him.

Chapter Thirty-Two

I t was the night of the show before she knew it. She took a half day at work and went home to get ready. She curled her hair and it fell in big soft curls just past her shoulders. She kept her makeup simple and used waterproof mascara because she had a feeling Lacey or her mother might make her cry. Not a sad cry but a happy cry at seeing them proud of her. The show was officially starting at seven pm and was catered.

She arrived early to see the whole place set up and to see if she could help. She wore flats and had her heels ready in the back room with her purse. She saw Matt had also arrived early. He looked really nervous. She felt really nervous but hoped she wasn't showing it. He came over to say hello and ask if she had talked to Gabe.

"No, when I saw the invitation I realized he would probably think you invited him" she replied.

"I thought that as well so even though you asked me not to, I did speak to him and made it clear that you invited him not me" he said clearly proud of himself.

"Did he sound happy that I was inviting him?" Jane

asked suddenly not caring anymore whether she looked nervous or not.

"He seemed very happy that you asked to be the one to invite him" Matt replied and then excusing himself went to ask Phil something.

Jane felt really nervous, she suddenly wished she had not foregone the idea of a sleeveless dress. She racked her brain trying to remember if she had reapplied deodorant when she went home to change. It was almost time, she realized, and went into the back room to change her shoes and fan her underarms. There goes all poise, she told herself and applied some bronze lip gloss. When she walked back into the room, she realized she had never asked Phil how she was supposed to act and what to do if people asked about her work.

She raced to find him and sensing a panicked artist, he got her a glass of champagne and told her to down it. It tickled her throat going down and once she finished it, he handed her another glass and told her to sip that one and mingle. He would bring over anyone who mattered. Otherwise she was free to hang out with her guests. If someone asked her about her work, she was to by all means talk about it but not too long, because this was an art show not a term paper. Taking her arm, he led her to the front area of the gallery, as guests began to arrive.

Her parents were amongst the first in, and after giving her a big hug, her father kissed her on the cheek. Lacey and Jack were not far behind them. Jane wanted to stay near the entrance to make sure she greeted everyone she had invited personally and to see Gabe as soon as he arrived. She watched all the guests stream in. All the men came in suits and ties and the women in dresses or posh suits.

Phil brought over an architect and his wife. They loved

the bridge concept and asked her questions about each one. She was still speaking with them when Gabe arrived. He looked so handsome in his suit and was carrying a bouquet of roses and pink heather. She excused herself and went to him. Nervously she went to hug him.

"Hey Jane" he said warmly "you look beautiful tonight. These are for you. The florist said the pink heather meant good luck."

"They are beautiful. Thank you so much for the flowers and for coming tonight" Jane said.

"It's kinda crazy you and Matt are showing together. When I got the invitation, I didn't believe it at first. I remember you talking about your love of art but I did not expect all this" Gabe replied.

"I'm really not sure if I'm supposed to stay here or if I can walk around yet" she confessed looking around for Matt. Catching her intent Gabe said

"Let me find Matt and I'll have him ask." He leaned in a kissed her cheek, then was gone.

She stood there with a dreamy smile on her face until he returned with Matt who was also brought Adam.

"Looks like we are free to walk around" Matt said.

"Do you want me to get you water for those?" Adam asked gesturing towards her flowers.

Jane nodded and Adam went off to get a vase. She hung out with Matt and Gabe until he came back. When he did she set them up on a table. Together Jane and Gabe moved from piece to piece.

Taking his hand, Jane said "I still really like you, but after everything that happened these past few months, I felt like I wasn't sure I liked me. Taking the time to do this made me feel grounded. I can't tell you how much it meant to me that you were cool about it."

"I gotta be honest it was rough, part of me was pretty

sure you were just going to bail but I really hoped you weren't" Gabe said leaning in to give her a kiss.

This felt so right she thought putting her arms around his neck. She didn't even care that they were in a room full of people, until she remembered that her parents were also here.

Pulling back she said "So, my parents are here and I've told them about you. Can I introduce you to them?"

"Sure" Gabe said taking her hand.

Lacey and Jack were talking to her parents when they walked up. Jane was about to introduce him when she was called to the center of the room with Matt to be presented to the attendees. They stood there as they were applauded. Once that was complete, Jane hurried back over to them. Gabe was talking to Lacey and they were all standing by the Nickel Bridge drawing Jane had dreamed of. Phil had placed a sold sign on it before the show had started. After introducing Gabe to her parents Jane had time to watch everyone look at her work. Phil came over excitedly to tell her two of her paintings had already sold. He then hurried away to speak to another patron.

"It's too bad this one has already sold" Gabe said motioning towards the Bridge from her dream. "It's my favorite."

"Mine too, and it's not really sold." Jane smiled "This one is staying with me."

Other Books by Carey Heywood

The Fix Series

Fix Her Up (Finley & Noah)

Fix Me Not (coming soon)

Him & Her Series

Him (book 1)

Her (book 2)

Them (book 3)

Sawyer Says (spin off)

Being Neighborly (spin off novella)

Carolina Days

The Other Side of Someday (Courtney & Clay)

Yesterday's Half Truths (Lindsay & Luke)

Chasing Daylight (McKenzie & Mitch)

Love Riddles

Why Now? (Kacey & Jake)

Why Lie? (Sydney & Heath)

Why Not? (Reilly & Trip)

Standalones

Better

Stages of Grace

Uninvolved

A Bridge of Her Own

Audiobooks

Him (also available on audible)

Her (also available on audible)

Better (also available on audible)

Acknowledgments

I want to thank everyone who helped and encouraged me along this journey. To Deena, Mary, Chrissy, Lisa, Judy, and Rachel who were some of my earliest readers. To Kate Dixon, I not only stole your last name for a character but unless can not think you enough for your advice.

To my mom, who was my very first reader/cheerleader and a special condolence to the bug she squished on page 158 of my first printed draft.

To Heather Markman at Traveler's Playground Press for her thoughtful editing. To Jamie Tibbs who was always available for me to vent to about completely made up people. Our daily walks helped inspire me to complete this endeavor more than you will ever know. Lastly, to my husband and children for their love and support.

www.ingramcontent.com/pod-product-compliance
Lightning Source LLC
Chambersburg PA
CBHW060415180626
46817CB00007B/2590